A BAD BUSINESS

ESSENTIAL STORIES

FYODOR DOSTOYEVSKY

TRANSLATED FROM THE RUSSIAN
BY NICOLAS PASTERNAK SLATER
AND MAYA SLATER

PUSHKIN PRESS CLASSICS

Pushkin Press
Somerset House, Strand
London WC2R ILA

"A Bad Business" was first published as "Skvernyi Anekdot"
(*Скверный анекдот*) in *Vremya* (*Time*), 1862

"The Crocodile" was first published as "Krokodil"
(*Крокодил*) in *Epokha* (*Epoch*), 1865

A Meek Creature was fi rst published as "Krotkaya"
(*Кроткая*) in *Dnevnik Pisatelya* (*A Writer's Diary*), 1876

"Conversations in a Graveyard (Bobok)" was first published
as "Bobok" (*Бобок*) in *Grazhdanin* (*The Citizen*), 1873

"The Heavenly Christmas Tree" was first published as "Malchik u Khrista na yolke"
(*Мальчик у Христа на ёлке*) in *Dnevnik Pisatelya* (*A Writer's Diary*), 1876

"The Peasant Marey" was first published as "Muzhik Marey"
(*Мужик Марей*) in *Dnevnik Pisatelya* (*A Writer's Diary*), 1876

This translation first published by Pushkin Press in 2021
This edition published in 2026

ISBN 13: 978-1-80533-206-0

A CIP catalogue record for this title is available from the British Library

The authorised representative in the EEA is
eucomply OÜ, Pärnu mnt. 139b-14, 11317, Tallinn, Estonia,
hello@eucompliancepartner.com, +33757690241

Designed and typeset by Tetragon, London
Printed and bound in the United Kingdom by Clays Ltd, Elcograf S.p.A.

Pushkin Press is committed to a sustainable future for our business, our readers and our planet. This book is made from paper from forests that support responsible forestry.

www.pushkinpress.com

1 3 5 7 9 8 6 4 2

CONTENTS

PUSHKIN PRESS CLASSICS

A BAD BUSINESS

ESSENTIAL STORIES

'The man more than any other who
has created modern prose'
JAMES JOYCE

'Nasty, violent, ironic, caustic,
and… extremely funny'
GUARDIAN

FYODOR DOSTOYEVSKY (1821–1881) trained as an engineer and began his literary career with translations. As punishment for engaging in progressive political discussion, he was subjected to a mock execution and sent into exile in Siberia in his twenties. Subsequently he worked exclusively as a writer, touring Europe and publishing novels and journalism. Addicted to gambling, he was often near starvation. His second, very happy marriage to typist Anna Snitkina helped to stabilize his manner of living, and with her practical assistance he went on to write several masterpieces of psychological and existential fiction. Novels such as *Crime and Punishment*, *The Idiot*, *The Brothers Karamazov* and *Notes from Underground* have earned him a lasting reputation as one of the dominant figures of world literature. Pushkin Press also publish his comic novel *The Friend of the Family*.

NICOLAS PASTERNAK SLATER, a bilingual nephew of Boris Pasternak, is a retired haemotologist. Published translations include Dostoyevsky's *Crime and Punishment* and Pasternak's *Doctor Zhivago*, as well as stories by Ivan Turgenev and Anton Chekhov. Most recently he translated Tolstoy's *Sevastopol Tales*, also published by Pushkin Press.

MAYA SLATER has published translations of Molière and other French writers, and co-translations with her husband Nicolas Pasternak Slater. She was formerly a Senior Research Fellow at Queen Mary University of London.

A BAD BUSINESS

A Story

T HIS BAD BUSINESS occurred at the very time when our beloved Fatherland, driven on with such irresistible force, and filled with such touchingly naïve enthusiasm, was just embarking on its regeneration, bearing with it all its valiant sons intent on their eager pursuit of new destinies and aspirations. It so happened, on a clear frosty winter evening—after eleven at night, in fact—that three extremely respectable gentlemen were seated in a comfortable, luxuriously appointed room in a splendid two-storey mansion on the Petersburg Side, engaged in an admirable and serious-minded conversation on a highly intriguing subject. All three gentlemen had the rank of general. They were sitting in three splendid cushioned armchairs round a little table, and as they talked they took quiet, luxurious sips of champagne. The bottle, in a silver ice bucket, stood on the table in front of them. They were there because their host, Privy Councillor Stepan Nikiforovich Nikiforov, an old bachelor of about sixty-five, was celebrating his house-warming in the house he had just bought; and this event happened to coincide with his birthday, which he never used to celebrate. Not that this celebration was all that splendid: as we have seen, there were only two guests, both of them former colleagues and subordinates of his in the service. One was Active State Councillor Semyon Ivanovich Shipulenko, and the other, also an active state councillor, was Ivan Ilyich Pralinsky. They had arrived about nine, had their tea, then moved on to the wine, and knew that at precisely eleven thirty they would have to set off for home. Their host had been a stickler for regularity all his life.

A word about the host. He had begun his career as a petty clerk with no backing, quietly carried on his daily grind for a full forty-five years, well aware how high he could rise in his job; he hated reaching for the stars, although he had already earned two of them, and particularly loathed expressing his personal opinion on any subject at all. He was honest—that is to say, he had never had occasion to do anything particularly dishonest; he was unmarried, because he was selfish; was far from stupid, but hated showing his intelligence;

particularly disliked shoddiness, and also fervour, which he regarded as moral shoddiness; and towards the end of his life he had totally sunk into a kind of delicious, indolent self-indulgence and systematic reclusiveness. He did sometimes go out to visit people of the better class, but ever since he was a young man he had always hated entertaining guests; and lately, when not playing patience, he would make do with the company of his dining-room clock, spending whole evenings placidly dozing in his armchair and listening to it ticking away under its glass dome on the mantelpiece. He looked extremely respectable and was well shaven, so that he seemed younger than his years and very well preserved, with the promise of living many years more; his manners were impeccably gentlemanly. His post was a pretty comfortable one, sitting on some committee and signing things. In short, he was thought to be a splendid fellow. He used to have only one passion, or rather one fervent longing, which was to have a house of his own, and one built as a gentleman's home rather than a capital investment. And now his wish had come true: he had found and bought himself a house on the Petersburg Side—true, it was quite a way out, but it had a garden, and the house was elegant. The new owner reasoned that it was all the better for being far out: he disliked entertaining, and if he himself had to drive out on a visit or to his office, he had a smart chocolate-coloured two-seater carriage, and his coachman Mikhey, and a pair of small but tough and handsome horses. All this he had acquired honestly by forty years of meticulous frugality, and it gladdened his heart.

That was why, once he had bought and moved into his new home, Stepan Nikiforovich's phlegmatic soul was filled with such joy that he actually invited guests to celebrate his birthday, which he had hitherto carefully kept secret from even his closest friends. In fact he had particular designs on one of his two guests. He himself had moved into the upper floor of his new house, but the lower floor, constructed and laid out in exactly the same way, was in want of a tenant. Stepan Nikiforovich was counting on Semyon Ivanovich Shipulenko, and in the course of this evening he had already twice alluded to the matter. But Semyon Ivanovich had not risen to the bait. He, too, was a man who had spent long years making his way in the service. He had black hair and side whiskers and a permanently bilious tinge to his face. He was a married man, a morose stay-at-home who terrorized his household. He performed his work with confidence, and he too knew exactly how high he would rise, and more importantly, the heights he would never reach. He had a good position, and was sitting tight. He viewed the latest reforms with a certain distaste, but was not particularly alarmed by them; he was very sure of himself, and when Ivan Ilyich Pralinsky held forth on these modern topics, he listened to him with malicious derision. But all three of them were a little tipsy by now, so even Stepan Nikiforovich condescended to engage in a mild argument with Pralinsky concerning the reforms. But a few words here about his Excellency Councillor Pralinsky, particularly as he is the principal hero of the story that follows.

Active State Councillor Ivan Ilyich Pralinsky had only been his Excellency for four months. In other words, he was a young general. Young in years, too— not more than forty-three, and he looked (and liked to look) younger still. He was a tall, handsome man, who dressed elegantly and prided himself on the refinement and respectability of his costume. He had an important decoration round his neck, which he wore with consummate style. Even as a child he had had the knack of acquiring the airs and graces of the beau monde, and now, still a bachelor, he dreamt of a wealthy bride from those circles. And he dreamt of many other things too, though he was far from stupid. At times he was a great talker, and even liked to pose as a parliamentarian. He came from a good family:

the son of a general, he had been brought up in the lap of luxury, dressed in velvet and fine linen even as a little boy. Educated at an aristocratic school, he had left it not much the wiser. Still, he had had a successful career and had risen to the rank of general. The authorities regarded him as a capable person, and had high hopes of him. Stepan Nikiforovich, under whom he had served from the start of his career and almost up to his promotion to general, had never regarded him as much of a practical man, and had no expectations of him whatsoever. But he liked the fact that Ivan Ilyich came from a good family, possessed a fortune (that is, a large block of rental properties with a manager), was related to influential people, and furthermore had a dignified air about him. Privately, Stepan Nikiforovich looked down on him as being too imaginative and frivolous. Ivan Ilyich himself sometimes felt that he was too vain and perhaps too touchy. Strangely enough, he was occasionally troubled by a morbidly tender conscience, and even a slight sense of remorse. From time to time he would acknowledge bitterly and with an aching heart that he was not really flying as high as he imagined. At such moments he would become depressed, particularly if his piles were troubling him, and say that his life was *une existence manquée*. He would—privately of course—lose faith in his parliamentary skills, calling himself a *parleur* and a *phraseur*. All this, of course, did him great credit, but it didn't stop him from holding his head high again half an hour later, reassuring himself more obstinately and conceitedly than ever, and resolving that he would make a name for himself yet, and become not only a great official but a statesman whom Russia would long remember. Sometimes he even dreamt of monuments. All this shows that Ivan Ilyich aimed high, though he kept his vague dreams and hopes hidden deep in his heart—and they actually rather scared him. In a word, he was a kind-hearted man, with the soul of a poet. In recent years his moments of morbid disillusionment had become more frequent. He had grown particularly irritable and touchy, always ready to take offence at anyone who disagreed with him. But the new Russian reforms had aroused great hopes in him. His promotion to general had done the rest. He livened up, and held his head high. He had begun to speak volubly and eloquently, discussing the very latest topics, which he had unexpectedly assimilated with amazing alacrity and now espoused with vigour. He looked out for opportunities to speak, drove around town, and in many places had already earned the reputation of an out-and-out liberal, which he found very flattering.

On this particular evening, after four glasses, he had let himself go more than ever. Having not seen Stepan Nikiforovich for some time, he was now keen to change his chief's mind on every subject, though he had hitherto always respected him and even obeyed him. For some reason he regarded him as a reactionary, and attacked him very fiercely. Stepan Nikiforovich scarcely replied, but just listened sardonically, although the topic interested him. Ivan Ilyich was becoming worked up, and in the heat of this imaginary dispute he sipped from his glass more often than he should. When this happened, Stepan Nikiforovich would take the bottle and top up his glass at once, which for some reason annoyed Ivan Ilyich, particularly as Semyon Ivanovich Shipulenko, whom he particularly despised and also feared as a spiteful cynic, was sitting to one side of him, maintaining a treacherous silence and smiling more often than he should. 'They seem to be taking me for a schoolboy'—the thought flashed through his head.

'No, sir, it was time, high time,' he went on vehemently, 'we've left it far too long, and to my mind a humane approach is the most important thing, a humane attitude towards our subordinates, remembering that they're human beings too. A humane attitude will rescue everything, it will carry everything . . .'

'He-he-he!' came from Semyon Ivanovich's direction.

'But why are you laying into us like this?' Stepan Nikiforovich finally protested, with a friendly smile. 'I must confess, Ivan Ilyich, I still can't make out what you're being good enough to explain to us. You talk about being humane. That means loving one's fellow man, does it?'

'Yes, loving one's fellow man, if you like. I—'

'Allow me. As far as I can see, that isn't the only thing. It's always been right to love one's fellow men. But the reforms go beyond that. There are questions that arise relating to the peasantry, the courts, the economy, government contracts, morality, and . . . and . . . and there's no end to them, these questions, and if you adopt them all at once, that could cause great . . . instability, so to speak. That's what's been worrying us, not just the question of being humane.'

'Yes, it all goes deeper,' remarked Semyon Ivanovich.

'I understand that perfectly well, and allow me to point out, Semyon Ivanovich, that I will certainly not accept that your understanding is superior to mine,' said Ivan Ilyich caustically and with unnecessary sharpness. 'Nevertheless, I shall make bold to point out to you too, Stepan Nikiforovich, that you haven't understood me either.'

'No, I haven't.'

'And yet I maintain, and everywhere promote the idea, that a humane attitude, specifically towards one's subordinates, from official to clerk, from clerk to domestic servant, from servant to peasant—a humane attitude, I say, can serve, as it were, as the cornerstone of the coming reforms, and of the reformation of things in general. Why? Because. Take this syllogism: I am humane, therefore I am loved. I am loved, therefore people feel confidence in me. They feel confidence, therefore they believe. They believe, therefore they love . . . or no, I mean to say, if they believe, then they will believe in the reforms, they'll grasp, as it were, the very nub of the matter, they will, as it were, embrace each other, in the moral sense, and settle the whole thing completely in a friendly way. Why are you laughing, Semyon Ivanovich? Don't you understand?'

Stepan Nikiforovich said nothing, but raised his eyebrows; he was surprised.

'I'm afraid I must have had a little too much to drink,' said Semyon Ivanovich venomously, 'so I'm slow on the uptake. Haven't got all my wits about me.'

Ivan Ilyich flinched.

'We won't hold out,' Stepan Nikiforovich suddenly pronounced after some brief reflection.

'What do you mean, we won't hold out?' demanded Ivan Ilyich, taken aback by Stepan Nikiforovich's unexpected and abrupt remark.

'Just that—we won't hold out.' Stepan Nikiforovich evidently did not want to expand further.

'You're not alluding to new wine in new wineskins, are you?' returned Ivan Ilyich ironically. 'Because no, I can certainly answer for myself.'

At that point the clock struck half past eleven.

'People sit on and on, but eventually they leave,' said Semyon Ivanovich, preparing to get up. But Ivan Ilyich forestalled him, got up from the table himself, and picked up his sable cap from the mantelpiece. He seemed offended.

'So, Semyon Ivanich, will you think it over?' asked Stepan Nikiforovich, seeing his guests to the door.

'About the little apartment, you mean? Yes, yes, I'll think about it.'

'Well, when you've made up your mind, let me know as soon as you can.'

'More business?' asked Ivan Ilyich Pralinsky, in an affable but rather ingratiating voice, twisting his cap in his hands. He felt ignored.

Stepan Nikiforovich raised his eyebrows and said nothing, making it clear that he was not detaining his guests. Semyon Ivanovich hastily took his leave.

'But . . . well . . . just as you like, then . . . if you can't understand a simple piece of courtesy,' Pralinsky thought, holding out his hand to Stepan Nikiforovich in a decidedly non-committal way.

In the hallway Ivan Ilyich wrapped himself up in his expensive lightweight fur coat, trying for some reason not to notice Semyon Ivanovich's shabby raccoon, and they set off down the stairs.

'The old man seemed offended,' said Ivan Ilyich to Semyon Ivanovich, who was saying nothing.

'No, why should he be?' replied the other, cool and composed.

'Servile creep!' thought Ivan Ilyich.

They went out to the front steps, and Semyon Ivanich's sleigh drew up, drawn by an unimpressive-looking colt.

'What on earth! Where the devil has Trifon got to with my carriage?' yelled Ivan Ilyich Pralinsky, not seeing his conveyance.

They looked this way and that, but there was no carriage. Stepan Nikiforovich's man had no idea. They asked Varlam, Semyon Ivanovich's driver, who told them that he'd been waiting there the whole time, and the carriage had been there too, but now it wasn't.

'A bad business!' said Semyon Ivanovich Shipulenko. 'Can I give you a lift?'

'Damned scoundrel!' yelled Pralinsky in a rage. 'That bastard was asking me to let him go to a wedding, over here on the Petersburg Side; apparently some woman friend of his was getting married, blast her eyes. I strictly forbade him to leave. And I bet you anything that's where he's gone!'

'That's exactly where he's gone, sir,' Varlam confirmed, 'and he promised he'd be back in a minute, I mean, he'd be here in time.'

'There you are! I could see it coming! Now he'll catch it!'

'Give him a proper thrashing or two at the police station, that'll teach him to obey orders,' remarked Semyon Ivanovich, wrapping himself in his rug.

'Please don't trouble yourself, Semyon Ivanich!'

'No, really, wouldn't you like a lift?'

'*Merci, bon voyage.*'

Semyon Ivanovich drove off, and Ivan Ilyich set off home along the wooden pavement in a state of intense irritation.

*

'Now you'll catch it, you villain! Just you wait! I'll walk home, just to make you feel it and take fright! He'll come back and find his master gone home on foot . . . bastard!'

Ivan Ilyich had never sworn that way before, but he was in a towering rage; besides which he was hearing noises in his head. He wasn't normally a drinker, so the five or six glasses in a row had quickly gone to his head. But the night was delightful. There was a frost, but the air was unusually quiet and still. The clear sky was filled with stars. The full moon flooded the earth with its soft silvery light. Everything was so lovely that by the time he had walked fifty steps, Ivan Ilyich had almost forgotten his troubles. He was feeling particularly pleased; when people are a bit tipsy, they can switch moods very quickly. He was even enjoying the sight of the boring little wooden houses on the deserted street.

'What a splendid idea it was to walk home,' he thought. 'It'll be a lesson to Trifon, and a pleasure for me. I really ought to do more walking. And what does it matter? I'll pick up a sleigh straight away on Bolshoi Prospect. What a beautiful night! Just look at all these little houses. I suppose simple people live there, clerks . . . shopkeepers, maybe . . . That Stepan Nikiforovich, now! What reactionaries they are, all those old fogeys! Yes, fogeys, *c'est le mot*. Though he's a clever fellow, he's got *bon sens*, a sober, practical understanding of things. But these old men, these old men! There's none of that . . . what d'you call it? . . Anyway, there's something missing. "We won't hold out!" What did he mean by that? He even got thoughtful when he said it. And he didn't understand me at all. How could he have not understood me? It's harder not to understand than to understand. The point is that I'm quite convinced, convinced in my soul. Humaneness . . . the love of one's fellow man. Restore a man to himself . . . reawaken his self-respect, and then . . . once the material's ready, get down to work. Obvious, I'd say! Yes sir! If you'll allow me, your Excellency, take this syllogism: we meet a clerk, let's say, a poor downtrodden clerk. "Well, and who are you?" Answer: "A clerk." Very well, a clerk; on we go: "What kind of a clerk?" Reply: this or that kind of a clerk. "Are you in the service?"— "Yes, I am!"—"Do you want to be happy?"—"Yes, I do!"—"What do you need to make you happy?"— "This and that."—"Why?"—"Because . . ." And here's a man who understands me after a couple of words; the man's mine, he's caught in my net, so to speak, and I can do anything I want with him, for his own good I mean. What a nasty man that Semyon Ivanovich is! And what an ugly mug! "Thrash him at the police station"; he said that on purpose. No, you're talking rubbish, thrash him yourself, but I won't; I'll punish Trifon with words, punish him with reproaches, and he'll mind that. As for thrashing with sticks, hmm . . . that depends, hmm . . . What about looking in at Emerance? Oh damn and blast these wretched planks!' he yelled, suddenly tripping up. 'And this is a capital city! Enlightenment! You could break your leg. Hmm. I can't stand that Semyon Ivanich; what an ugly mug! He was laughing at me, back then, when I said they'd embrace each other, in the moral sense. So they'll embrace each other—what's it to do with you? I shan't be embracing you, anyway—I'd rather hug a peasant . . . If I meet a peasant, I'll talk to him, peasant or not. Actually, I was drunk, maybe I didn't express myself properly. Maybe I'm not expressing myself properly now either . . . Hmm. I'll never drink any more. You talk your head off in the evening, and next day you wish you hadn't. But I'm walking along all right, I'm not staggering around . . . Anyway, they're villains, the lot of them!'

Such were Ivan Ilyich's fragmentary and incoherent thoughts as he strode along the pavement. The fresh air had its effect on him; it got him going, so to speak. In another five minutes he would have calmed down and felt sleepy. But now, barely a couple of steps from Bolshoi Prospect, he heard the sound of music. He turned round to look. Across the road was a long, low, tumbledown wooden house, with a wild party in full swing indoors; fiddles wailing, a double bass scraping, a flute whistling a light-hearted quadrille. A crowd had gathered outside, under the windows, mostly women in padded coats and headscarves, trying their very best to peep through the cracks in the shutters and see what was going on. The people indoors were obviously having a great time. The thump of dancing feet could be heard across the street. Ivan Ilyich saw a policeman not far off, and approached him.

'Whose house is that, my man?' he asked, letting his expensive fur coat fall open a little, just wide enough for the policeman to make out the imposing medal round his neck.

'Clerk Pseldonimov, registrar, sir,' replied the policeman, instantly drawing himself up as he saw the decoration.

'Pseldonimov? Hah! Pseldonimov! What's he up to? Getting married?'

'Yes, your Honour, marrying the daughter of a titular councillor. Mlekopitaev, Titular Councillor . . . served on the council. The house comes with the bride, sir.'

'So this isn't Mlekopitaev's house any more, but Pseldonimov's?'

'That's it, your Honour. It was Mlekopitaev's, but now it's Pseldonimov's.'

'Hmm. The reason I'm asking, my man, is that I'm his chief. I'm the general in charge of the same department where Pseldonimov works.'

'Yes, your Excellency, sir . . .' The policeman had drawn himself up to his full height now, while Ivan Ilyich seemed to become pensive. He stood there, wondering . . .

Yes indeed. Pseldonimov was in his department, in fact in his own office. He was a minor official, on around ten roubles a month. Since Pralinsky had only taken over his office very recently, he might not have remembered all his staff so clearly—but he remembered Pseldonimov, just because of his surname. It had caught his eye as soon as he saw it, so he had been curious to take a closer look at the owner of such a surname. And now he remembered a very young man, scrawny, underfed, with a long hooked nose and pale wispy hair, wearing an impossible uniform coat and unmentionables that were so impossible that they were actually indecent. He recalled the thought that had flashed through his mind then: shouldn't he award the poor wretch a holiday bonus of ten roubles to spruce himself up? But as the poor man had such a glum face and such an unprepossessing and repellent expression, that kindly thought had evaporated of its own accord, and Pseldonimov never got his bonus. Ivan Ilyich had been all the more astounded, no more than a week before, when Pseldonimov requested permission to marry. He remembered not having had time to look into the matter properly, so that it was all settled in a hasty, offhand way. Even so, he could recall very precisely that Pseldonimov's bride was to come with a dowry of a wooden house and four hundred roubles in cash; he had been surprised at that at the time, and had even made a mild joke about the clash between the two names of Pseldonimov and Mlekopitaeva.* He distinctly remembered all that.

And as he recalled it, he became more and more thoughtful. We all know that whole trains of thought can sometimes pass through our minds in an instant, like mere sensations, without being translated into human language or certainly not into literary language. But we shall try to translate our hero's unspoken sensations, offering the reader at least the substance of

* The surname Pseldonimov is an obvious corruption of the Russian word for 'pseudonym'. The name Mlekopitaeva comes from the Russian word for a mammal, *mlekopitayuscheye*.

them, their most essential and realistic elements. After all, many of our sensations, when translated into everyday language, come to seem utterly unreal. That is why they never get expressed, though we all experience them. Naturally Ivan Ilyich's sensations were somewhat incoherent—but you know why that was.

'Just think,' there flashed through his mind, 'we go on talking and talking, but when we get down to business, there's nothing to show for it. Take this Pseldonimov, for instance: he's just come back from his wedding, all excited, full of hope, eager to taste the . . . This is one of the most blissful days of his life . . . Now he's looking after his guests, setting up the feast—a modest one, a poor one, but merry, joyful, heartfelt . . . What if he knew that at this very minute, I, I myself, his superior, his chief, was standing right here outside his house, listening to his music! Well, so what would he really feel? No, how would he feel, if I suddenly took it into my head to walk in? Hmm . . . Naturally he'd be frightened at first, he'd be speechless with embarrassment. I'd be in the way, I might spoil the whole occasion, perhaps . . . Yes, that's what would happen if any other general were to walk in, but not me . . . That's how it is, with anyone but me.

'Yes, Stepan Nikiforovich! You didn't understand me this evening, but I'm a living example for you.

'Yes, sir. Here we are, all shouting about humane attitudes, but to perform a heroic act, a true exploit—that's beyond our powers.

'What sort of heroic act? Just this. Think about it: in the present state of relations between different classes of society, if I, I myself, were to present myself after midnight at the wedding feast of my subordinate, a registrar on ten roubles a month—why, that would be crazy, it would be the world turned upside down, the last days of Pompeii, pure Bedlam. Nobody would understand. Stepan Nikiforovich would die without ever understanding. Didn't he say: we won't hold out? Yes, that goes for you others, old men, stagnant and paralysed as you are—but I—will—hold—out! I'll transform the last day of Pompeii into the most delightful day for my subordinate, I'll turn a crazy action into a normal one, patriarchal, lofty and moral. How? Like this. Kindly listen.

'Well then ... just suppose ... I go in; everyone's amazed, the dancing stops, they all look at me wild-eyed, backing away. Yes, but now I show myself: I go straight over to frightened Pseldonimov, with the friendliest of smiles, and I explain in the simplest possible terms: "Thus and thus, I've been visiting his Excellency Stepan Nikiforovich; I suppose you know he lives around here ..." And then I allude, in a humorous way, you know, to my adventure with Trifon.

After Trifon, I go on to how I left on foot . . . "Well, and I heard music, and asked a policeman, and found out that you, my man, were getting married. So, I thought, why not drop in on my subordinate, have a look at all my staff having a good time, and . . . and getting married. You won't throw me out, I suppose!" Throw me out! What a word for a subordinate! How could he possibly throw me out! I imagine he'll be out of his mind, he'll rush headlong to sit me down in an armchair, trembling with delight, at first he won't know if he's on his head or his heels!

'Now what could be simpler and more elegant than that? And why did I go in? That's another question! That's the moral aspect of the business, if you like. That's the nub of it!

'Hmm . . . What was I thinking about, again? Oh yes!

'Well of course, they'll sit me down with the principal guest, some titular councillor, or a relative, some red-nosed retired staff captain . . . Gogol wrote marvellous descriptions of those oddballs. Well, they introduce me to the bride, naturally, and I compliment her, and reassure the guests. Ask them not to stand on ceremony, but enjoy themselves, carry on dancing . . . I make jokes, I laugh, in short I'm affable and charming. I'm always affable and charming when I'm pleased with myself . . . Hmm . . . the point is, I believe I'm still a bit . . . not drunk, I mean, but . . .

'Naturally, being a gentleman, I shall be on an equal footing with them, and shan't expect any special marks of . . . But morally, morally, that's another matter: they'll understand and appreciate that. My action will reawaken their nobler feelings . . . I'll stay half an hour . . . perhaps even an hour. Of course I'll leave before supper, while they're bustling around, baking, roasting, they'll bow low to me, but I'll just drink a glass, wish them well, but refuse supper. Business, I'll say. And as soon as I say the word "business", they'll all instantly put on stern, respectful expressions. That'll be a delicate way of reminding them that there's a difference between me and them. Like between heaven and earth. Not that I want to rub that in, but one has to . . . even in the moral sense, it has to be done, whatever you say. Although I'll have a smile, in fact I'll give a laugh, and everyone will cheer up straight away . . . I'll have another joke with the bride; hmm . . . in fact here's what I'll do, I'll give a hint that I'll be back in just nine months' time, to stand godfather, heh-heh! She's bound to have given birth by then. They breed like rabbits. Well, and everyone will burst out laughing, and the bride will blush; I'll give her a warm kiss on the forehead, in fact I'll give her my blessing, and . . . and next day everyone in the office will know about my exploit. But next day I shall be stern again, and exacting again, even implacable; but by then everyone will know what I'm really like. They'll know my heart, they'll know my true nature: "He's strict, as a chief; but as a man, he's an angel!" And so I'll have won them over—just one ordinary little act, which you'd never have dreamt of, and now they're mine: I'm their father, they're my children . . . Come on, your Excellency, Stepan Nikiforovich, you go and try doing something like that!

'. . . Do you realize, do you understand that Pseldonimov will tell his children that the general himself joined in the feast, and actually drank at his wedding! I mean, those children will tell their own children, and those will tell their grandchildren, the sacred story of the grand personage, the statesman (for I'll be all that by then), did them the great honour . . . et cetera et cetera. Why, I shall be morally elevating that humiliated man, restoring him to himself . . . Just think, he only gets ten roubles a month! . . Why, if I repeat this action five times, or ten times, or something of the sort, I'll make myself popular everywhere . . . I'll have a special place in all their hearts, and the devil alone knows what that could lead to, all that popularity!'

Such, more or less, were the thoughts of Ivan Ilyich (you see, dear readers, a man may say all sorts of things to himself, particularly when he's in a somewhat eccentric frame of mind). All these considerations slipped through his mind in the space of half a minute or so, and of course he might have confined himself to these dreams, and having put Stepan Nikiforovich to shame in his imagination, he might have gone quietly home and put himself to bed. And it would have been just as well if he had. But this was an eccentric moment, and that was the whole problem.

As luck would have it, just at that very moment the smug faces of Stepan Nikiforovich and Semyon Ivanovich rose up in his fevered imagination.

'We won't hold out!' repeated Stepan Nikiforovich, with a lofty smile.

'Heh-heh-heh!' Semyon Ivanovich took him up, with his nastiest smirk.

'Let's just see whether we hold out or not!' said Ivan Ilyich in a resolute voice, and a hot flush spread over his face. Stepping off the wooden pavement, he strode firmly across the road, straight over to the house of his subordinate, Registrar Pseldonimov.

*

His star drew him on. He walked boldly in through the open gate, disdainfully kicking aside a shaggy, husky-voiced little dog that hurled itself at his feet, barking gruffly more for form's sake than with any thought of aggression. He walked along some wooden planking up to a covered porch, which stood like a sentry box at the entrance to the yard, and climbed three rickety wooden steps to a narrow entrance. Here, although there was some sort of tallow candle end burning in the corner, or perhaps a little oil lamp, that did not stop him planting his left foot, galosh and all, into a galantine placed outside to cool. He bent down curiously to look, and saw two more dishes with jellies of some sort, and two moulds presumably containing blancmange. He was a bit embarrassed by the squashed galantine, and for a fraction of a second he wondered whether he shouldn't just slip away on the spot? But he decided that would be too mean-spirited, and reflecting that no one had seen him and no one could possibly suspect him, he quickly wiped all the traces off his galosh, groped for the felt-lined door, opened it and found himself in a tiny vestibule. One half of it was piled high with overcoats, winter jackets, cloaks, bonnets, scarves and galoshes; the other half was occupied by the musicians: two fiddles, a flute and a double bass, four players in all, brought in from the street, needless to say. They were sitting at a bare wooden table by the light of a single tallow candle, scraping away at the last figure of the quadrille as though their lives depended on it. Through the open doorway one could make out the dancers in a room full of dust, smoke and fumes, amid an atmosphere of wild gaiety, loud laughter, shouts and women's shrieks. The men were stomping about like a troop of horses. All this pandemonium was dominated by the voice of the master of ceremonies, an extremely laid-back, not to say unbuttoned, gentleman, shouting 'Cavaliers step forward, *chaîne de dames, balancez!*', and so on. In some agitation, Ivan Ilyich shed his overcoat and galoshes, and came into the room cap in hand. It must be said that he was no longer thinking straight.

At first no one noticed him: everyone was taken up by the end of the dance. Ivan Ilyich stood there bewildered, unable to make out anything in the chaotic medley before him. Ladies' gowns flashed past, and gentlemen with cigarettes between their teeth ... Some lady's blue-grey shawl floated by, catching him on the nose. Close behind her came a wildly excited medical student with a shock of unruly hair, barging straight into him as he passed. He glimpsed an officer from some unit, tall as a beanpole. Someone else swept past, stamping in time with all the others and yelling in an unnaturally shrill voice 'He-e-e-ey, Pseldonimushka!' The floor felt sticky under his feet; it must have been waxed. The room, not a particularly small one, was packed with thirty-odd guests.

But a minute later the quadrille was over, and what happened next, almost straight away, was exactly as Ivan Ilyich had imagined it when he stood dreaming on the plank walkway. A kind of murmur, a strange whisper passed among the guests who had been dancing, even before they had time to catch their breath and wipe the sweat off their faces. All eyes, all faces at once turned towards the new guest. Then everyone began to draw back and move away. Those who had noticed nothing were tugged by their clothes and given explanations. Then they looked round and immediately backed off with the rest. Ivan Ilyich still stood in the doorway, not moving a step forward, so that an open space formed between him and the guests, growing wider and wider and revealing the floor strewn with countless sweet wrappers, tickets and cigarette ends. Now someone stepped timidly out into this empty space: a man in uniform, with unruly fair hair and a hooked nose. He moved forward, shoulders bent, eyeing the unexpected guest with the exact expression of a dog whose master has summoned it to give it a kick.

'Good evening, Pseldonimov—recognize me?' said Ivan Ilyich, instantly feeling that he had said that very awkwardly. He also felt that he might at that very moment be doing something dreadfully stupid.

'Y-y-your Ex-ex-cellency!' stammered Pseldonimov.

'Well, yes indeed. I've dropped in on you by pure chance, my boy, as you may well imagine . . .'

But Pseldonimov clearly couldn't imagine a thing. He stood there, eyes popping, in the most ghastly bewilderment.

'You won't throw me out, I suppose . . . Pleased or not, you have to make a guest welcome! . .' Ivan Ilyich went on, feeling that he himself was becoming pathetically embarrassed, that he wanted to smile but couldn't, and that the humorous account of Stepan Nikiforovich and Trifon he had planned to give was becoming more and more unthinkable. But Pseldonimov seemed wilfully unable to recover from his daze, and went on staring at Ivan Ilyich like an absolute idiot. Ivan Ilyich winced: he felt that if this went on a minute longer, it would end in absolute mayhem.

'Perhaps I'm in the way . . . I'll leave!' he just managed to bring out, and the right side of his mouth started twitching . . .

Pseldonimov came to his senses . . .

'Your Excellency, I beg you . . . The honour . . .' he stuttered, bowing hurriedly, 'Please be so good as to take a seat . . .' And pulling himself together even more, he motioned him with both hands towards a sofa, where a table had been shifted aside for the dancing.

Ivan Ilyich mentally breathed a sigh of relief, and lowered himself onto the sofa; someone rushed up at once to move the table back. He took a quick look round and saw that he was the only one seated, everyone else was standing, even the ladies. A bad sign. But it was too soon to remind or reassure them. The guests were still holding back; only Pseldonimov stood there before him, bent double, as bewildered as ever, and far from smiling. Things were looking bad; in fact our hero was so despondent at that moment that his sudden descent on his subordinate, undertaken in the spirit of Haroun al-Rashid, might well have ranked as a heroic exploit. But now a little figure turned up next to Pseldonimov and began bowing. With inexpressible pleasure, indeed with positive happiness, Ivan Ilyich at once recognized Akim Petrovich Zubikov, chief clerk in his office. He was not well acquainted with him, of course, but he knew him to be a businesslike man of few words. He got up at once and held out his hand to Akim Petrovich—his whole hand, not just two fingers. Akim Petrovich took it in both his hands, with profoundest reverence. The general was triumphant: the situation was saved.

For indeed, Pseldonimov was now, as it were, no longer the second party but the third. That story could now be told directly to the chief clerk, treating him willy-nilly as an acquaintance, even a close one, while Pseldonimov could be left to stand there speechless and quake with reverence. The proprieties would be observed. But the story had to be told— Ivan Ilyich could feel that. He could see that all the guests were expecting something; the whole household had crowded together in the two doorways, almost climbing over one another to have a look at him and hear what he had to say. The worst of it was that the chief clerk was still being too stupid to sit down.

'Come on, do!' said Ivan Ilyich, gesturing awkwardly at the place next to him on the sofa.

'It's all right, sir . . . I'll be fine here . . .' and Akim Petrovich quickly sat down on a chair almost as soon as it was put out for him by Pseldonimov, who obstinately remained on his feet.

'Just imagine what happened,' began Ivan Ilyich, addressing Akim Petrovich alone; his voice was a little unsteady, but quite nonchalant. He was even drawling out his words, emphasizing individual syllables, pronouncing his 'ah-' sounds as 'eh-'; in short, he was well aware of being affected, but couldn't control it.

Some external force was at work. He was excruciatingly conscious of many different things at that moment.

'Can you imagine, I've only just come from visiting Stepan Nikiforovich Nikiforov—you may have heard of him, the privy councillor. I mean . . . on that special commission . . .'

Akim Petrovich inclined his whole body forward respectfully, as if to say, 'Naturally, of course I know about him, sir.'

'He's your neighbour now,' went on Ivan Ilyich, turning for one moment to address Pseldonimov, to relax the atmosphere and preserve good manners. But he quickly turned his head away again, having seen in an instant in Pseldonimov's eyes that he couldn't care less.

'The old fellow, as you know, has been going on all his life about buying himself a house . . . Well, now he's bought one. And a very nice one too. Yes . . . And today was his birthday, though he's never celebrated it before, in fact he kept it secret from us, too stingy to give a party, heh-heh! But now he's so pleased with his new house, he invited me and Semyon Ivanovich. You know, Shipulenko, I mean.'

Akim Petrovich bowed again. Bowed eagerly! Ivan Ilyich felt a little reassured. He had been beginning to think that the chief clerk must have guessed that just then he was his Excellency's only hope. That would have been worse than anything.

'Well, the three of us sat there, he served us champagne, we talked business together . . . this and that . . . questions of . . . We even had an ar-gu-ment . . . Heh-heh!'

Akim Petrovich raised his eyebrows deferentially.

'But never mind that. So eventually I said goodbye, he's a punctual old soul, goes to bed early, you know, in his old age. So I go out—and my Trifon's nowhere to be seen! That worries me, and I ask around, "Where's Trifon gone with my carriage?" And it turns out he'd been hoping I'd stay late, and had gone off to the wedding of some friend of his, or his sister . . . or someone, Lord knows who. Somewhere here on the Petersburg Side. And he'd gone off with the carriage too.' Once again the general glanced at Pseldonimov, for form's sake. The host instantly bent double, but not at all in the way the general would have liked. 'No sympathy, no heart,' passed through the general's mind.

'My word!' said Akim Petrovich, much impressed. A soft murmur of surprise ran through the company.

'Imagine my situation . . .' (Ivan Ilyich glanced at them all). 'Nothing to be done, so I set off on foot. I thought I'd stroll along to Bolshoi Prospect and find myself a cab . . . heh-heh!'

'Hee-hee-hee!' Akim Petrovich echoed him respectfully. Another murmur, but a more cheerful one. Just then the glass chimney of a wall lamp cracked with a loud report. Someone eagerly ran over to deal with it. Pseldonimov gave a start and looked sternly at the lamp, but the general ignored it completely, and all was calm again.

'So I walked along . . . and it was such a beautiful quiet night. Suddenly I hear music, stamping feet, dancing. I ask a policeman: turns out Pseldonimov's getting married. So, my boy, you're throwing a ball for the whole of the Petersburg Side, are you? Ha-ha!' he finished, turning back to Pseldonimov.

'Hee-hee-hee! Oh yes . . .' echoed Akim Petrovich. The guests began moving around again, but the stupidest thing was that Pseldonimov—although he bowed once more—still didn't give the faintest smile. As though he was made of wood. 'Why's he such a fool?' wondered Ivan Ilyich. 'That would have been the moment for a smile, the ass, then everything would have been all right.' He was burning with impatience. 'So I thought—why not drop in on my clerk? He won't turn me out, after all . . . Like it or not, you have to make a guest welcome. Please excuse me, my boy. If

I'm in the way, I'll leave . . . I only dropped in to have a look . . .'

But bit by bit the room was coming to life again. Akim Petrovich looked at him, simpering as if to say, 'How could you possibly be in the way, your Excellency?' The guests began to move around, showing the first signs of being at ease. Almost all the ladies were sitting down again. A good sign, a positive sign. The boldest of them were fanning themselves with their handkerchiefs. One of them, in a worn velvet dress, said something in a purposely loud voice. The officer she was addressing wanted to answer her loudly too, but as they were the only two loud ones, he gave up. The men, mostly government clerks, apart from two or three students, exchanged glances as though prompting each other to loosen up; they cleared their throats, and even tapped their feet on the floor a little. No one was being particularly shy any more, but they were rough types and almost all directing hostile glances at this individual who had burst in on them to stop them having a good time. The officer, now ashamed of his cowardice, began sidling towards the table.

'Tell me, my boy, if you will—what's your full name?' Ivan Ilyich asked Pseldonimov.

'Porfiry Petrovich, your Excellency,' he replied, goggle-eyed as if he were on parade.

'Well, Porfiry Petrovich, do introduce me to your young wife, will you? If you'll lead the way . . . I'll . . .'

And he made a move to get up. But Pseldonimov rushed out at full tilt to the parlour. His bride had been standing right in the doorway, but as soon as she heard herself mentioned, she hid out of sight. A minute later Pseldonimov led her in by the hand. Everyone made way for them. Ivan Ilyich solemnly rose to his feet and addressed her with his most affable smile.

'Very, very glad to meet you,' he pronounced, with a most urbane inclination of the head, 'and particularly on a day like this . . .'

And he smiled the slyest of smiles. The ladies fluttered approvingly.

'*Charmée*,' said the lady in the velvet dress, almost audibly.

The bride was worthy of Pseldonimov—a thin little lady of no more than seventeen, pale, with a very small face and a pointed nose. Her little eyes darted this way and that, quite unembarrassed; in fact they had a piercing, almost spiteful look. Pseldonimov had evidently not chosen her for her beauty. She was in a white muslin dress over a pink underdress. Her neck was skinny, her body like a chicken's, with projecting bones. When the general greeted her, she couldn't say a word in reply.

'How very attractive she is,' he went on in an undertone, as if addressing Pseldonimov alone, though making sure that the bride could hear him too. But Pseldonimov once more said not a word, and did not even move his body. Ivan Ilyich had the impression that there was something cold in his eyes, something hidden, a private thought, a special, malignant thought. And yet he absolutely had to draw out some feeling from the man. That was what he had come for.

'What a couple!' he thought. 'Although . . .'

And he turned back to the bride, who was now sitting beside him on the sofa. But in answer to his two or three questions he got no more than a 'yes' and a 'no', and barely even that.

'If only she'd even get embarrassed,' he thought to himself, 'then I could begin to tease her. But as it is, the position's hopeless.' And Akim Petrovich, too, was being obstinately silent—no doubt out of stupidity, but it was still unpardonable.

'My friends! Am I perhaps interfering with your enjoyment?' he asked the whole company. He could feel his very palms sweating.

'No, sir . . . not to worry, your Excellency, we'll start again in a minute, but just now . . . we're cooling off a bit,' replied the officer. The bride gave him an approving look. The officer was a young man, in the uniform of some military unit. Pseldonimov was still standing there, leaning forward, and seemed to be sticking his hooked nose out even more. He was watching and listening, like a footman holding a fur coat while waiting for his masters to conclude their farewells. This comparison occurred to Ivan Ilyich himself: he was beginning to lose his head; he felt awkward, dreadfully awkward—as if the ground was slipping away beneath his feet; as if he was shut in somewhere with no way out; as if he was in the dark.

*

All at once everyone stood aside, and a short, sturdy middle-aged woman appeared, dressed in her simple best, with a big shawl over her shoulders, pinned at the throat, and a cap that she seemed unused to wearing. She was carrying a small round tray bearing a full but uncorked bottle of champagne and two glasses, no more and no less. The bottle was evidently intended for just two guests.

The woman made straight for the general.

'Do please forgive us, your Excellency,' she began with a bow, 'but since you have been so kind as to do my son this honour, and have condescended to attend his wedding, we ask you graciously to drink the happy couple's health. Don't disdain us, please do us this honour.'

Ivan Ilyich seized on her as his salvation. She was far from elderly—forty-five or forty-six, no older. But she had such a kindly, rosy-cheeked face, so round and open-hearted and Russian, and such a friendly smile, and she bowed so simply, that Ivan Ilyich was almost reassured, and began to feel hopeful again.

'So y-y-you are the p-parent of your son?' he asked, rising from the sofa.

'Yes, my mother, your Excellency,' mumbled Pseldonimov, stretching his long neck and thrusting his nose forward again.

'Ah! Very pleased, ve-ry pleased to make your acquaintance.'

'Do please accept this, your Excellency, don't refuse us.'

'With the very greatest pleasure indeed.'

The tray was placed on the table and Pseldonimov hastened to pour out the wine. Ivan Ilyich, still standing, picked up a glass.

'I am especially, especially glad of this chance to let you know . . . to let you know . . . on this occasion . . . In a word, as your chief . . . . I wish you,' (addressing the bride), 'and you too, my friend Porfiry,—I wish you perfect, complete and lasting happiness.'

And he drank off his glass with sincere feeling—his seventh that evening. Pseldonimov was looking serious, even sullen. The general was developing an agonizing hatred of him.

'And here's that ten-foot beanpole'—he glanced at the officer—'still hanging around. Why couldn't he have shouted "hurrah!"? That would have got things going . . . got things going . . .'

'You too, Akim Petrovich—do have a glass and drink their health,' said the mother to the chief clerk. 'You're my boy's boss, he's under you. Look after my young son, I ask you as a mother. And don't forget us in times to come, my dear Akim Petrovich, such a kind man as you are.'

'What lovely people these old Russian women are!' thought Ivan Ilyich. 'Cheered us all up. I've always been fond of the common people . . .'

At this point another tray was carried to the table by a maid in a crackling new chintz dress, never yet washed, and a crinoline. The tray was almost too huge for her to manage. On it were countless little plates of apples, sweets, candied fruit, fruit jellies, walnuts and so forth. It had been placed in the parlour for all the guests to sample, especially the ladies. But now it was brought to the general alone.

'Please don't turn us down, your Excellency. We're delighted to offer you what we have,' repeated the old lady with a bow.

'By all means . . .' said Ivan Ilyich, picking up a walnut and cracking it between his fingers; he actually enjoyed doing that, and had resolved to win popularity whatever it took.

Suddenly the bride giggled.

'What is it?' asked Ivan Ilyich with a smile, pleased to see a sign of life.

'It's Ivan Kostenkinich here, he's making me laugh,' she replied, lowering her eyes.

The general could now pick out a fair-haired young man, exceedingly handsome, who was sitting unobtrusively on a chair on the far side of the sofa and whispering to Madame Pseldonimova. He stood up, looking very young and very shy.

'I was telling the lady about a "dream book", your Excellency,' he muttered almost apologetically.

'What sort of a dream book?' asked Ivan Ilyich indulgently.

'There's a new dream book, sir, a literary one, sir. I was telling the lady, if someone dreams about Mr Panaev, that means he'll spill coffee on his shirt front, sir.'

'How naïve!' thought Ivan Ilyich, almost crossly. The young man had blushed scarlet as he spoke, but nevertheless was incredibly pleased to have said his piece about Mr Panaev.

'Well, yes, yes, so I've heard,' replied his Excellency.

'No, here's something better still,' said another voice, right next to Ivan Ilyich. 'There's a new encyclopaedia being published; well, they say Mr Kraevsky will be writing articles, and satirical literature . . .'

This speaker was also a young man, but not a bashful one—in fact he had quite a cocky look, with his white waistcoat and gloves, hat in hand. He had not been dancing, but merely looking on superciliously, because he was on the staff of the satirical magazine *The Firebrand* and gave himself airs accordingly. He had happened to drop in on the wedding, having been invited by Pseldonimov as an honoured guest. The two were close friends who had been living together in poverty and lodging in the cramped corner of some German woman's flat only a year before. He did drink vodka, however, and for that purpose had already disappeared more than once into a cosy back room to which everyone knew the way. The general detested him on sight.

'And the reason that's funny,' the fair-haired youth eagerly interrupted—the one who had been talking about shirt fronts, and at whom the journalist in the white waistcoat was now darting black looks—'the reason it's funny, your Excellency, is because the writer thinks that Mr Kraevsky can't spell, and thinks that "satire" is spelt with a Y, not an I.'

But the poor youth could barely get to the end of his sentence. He saw from the general's eyes that he had known all this for ages, because the general himself seemed embarrassed now, probably because he knew it. The young man felt utterly humiliated, managed to slip quickly out of sight, and spent the rest of the evening feeling very low. But the cocky young man from *The Firebrand* moved even closer to the general, and seemed to want to sit down next to him. Such free and easy manners struck Ivan Ilyich as uncalled-for.

'Yes! Do tell me, please, Porfiry,' he began, to break the silence, 'how is it—I've always wanted to ask you this in person—how is it that you're called Pseldonimov instead of Pseudonymov? I suppose you're really Pseudonymov, aren't you?'

'I don't rightly know, your Excellency,' replied Pseldonimov.

'It must have happened when his father entered the service, they made a mix-up in his papers, and since then he's always been Pseldonimov,' suggested Akim Petrovich. 'That does happen.'

'Un-doubt-ed-ly so,' the general replied eagerly, 'un-doubt-ed-ly so, because, see for yourself: Pseudonymov, that comes from the literary word "pseudonym". Whereas Pseldonimov doesn't mean anything.'

'Stupidity, sir,' added Akim Petrovich.

'That's—what exactly do you mean, stupidity?'

'The Russian people, sir; they sometimes mix up spellings out of stupidity, and pronounce words in their own way. Ninvalid, they say, for instance, instead of invalid, sir.'

'Well, yes . . . ninvalid. Ha-ha-ha . . .'

'Mumber, they say, too, your Excellency,' barked the tall officer, who had long been itching to make his mark.

'What do you mean, mumber?'

'Mumber, instead of number, your Excellency.'

'Ah yes, mumber . . . instead of number . . . Well, yes, yes . . . ha-ha-ha! . .' Ivan Ilyich had to give the officer a chuckle too.

The officer straightened his tie.

'And another thing they say is "He done it",' put in the journalist on *The Firebrand*. But his Excellency did his best not to hear him. He wasn't about to chuckle for everybody.

'He done it, instead of he did it,' insisted the journalist, visibly irritated.

Ivan Ilyich gave him a black look.

'What are you going on for?' whispered Pseldonimov to the journalist.

'What do you mean? I'm talking. Can't a man

talk?' the journalist protested in a whisper. But he said no more, and left the room in silent fury.

He went straight through to the cosy back room, where a little table had been prepared for gentlemen dancers at the very beginning of the evening. Laid out on a Yaroslavl tablecloth were two kinds of vodka, herring, slices of pressed caviar and a bottle of extra-strong Russian sherry. With rage in his heart, he was on the point of pouring himself some vodka when the tousle-headed medical student ran in; he was the prize dancer and cancan artist at Pseldonimov's ball. He launched himself at the decanter with greedy haste.

'Just starting!' he said, quickly helping himself. 'Come and watch. I'll be doing a solo upside down, and after dinner I'll risk doing the fish dance. That'll be very appropriate for a wedding. A sort of friendly hint to Pseldonimov ... She's a jolly girl, that Kleopatra Semyonovna, you can try anything on with her.'

'He's a reactionary,' answered the journalist morosely, tossing off his glass of vodka.

'Who's a reactionary?'

'Him—that man, the one they served all those sweets to. He's a reactionary, I'm telling you.'

'Oh, get along!' muttered the student, rushing out of the room as he heard the quadrille striking up.

Left to himself, the journalist poured himself some more vodka to boost his self-confidence and independence, drank it down and had a bite to eat. Never had Active State Councillor Ivan Ilyich made himself a fiercer enemy, or one more implacably bent on revenge, than this journalist on *The Firebrand* whom he had so slighted—especially after those two glasses of vodka. Alas! Ivan Ilyich had no idea. Nor did his Excellency suspect one other crucial fact, which coloured all his subsequent relations with the guests: although he had given what he regarded as an adequate, indeed detailed explanation of why he had turned up at his clerk's wedding, his explanation had not actually satisfied anyone, and the guests were still embarrassed. But suddenly, as if by magic, everything changed: the whole company felt reassured and prepared to have fun, laugh, squeal and dance about, just as if the uninvited guest hadn't been there at all. This was because of a rumour, a whisper, a piece of news that suddenly spread about, no one knew where from, to the effect that the guest seemed to be . . . rather pickled. And although at first glance that looked like a terrible slander, bit by bit it began to seem true, and everything became clear. What was more, everyone suddenly began to feel incredibly free. And that was the moment when the quadrille began—the last one before supper, the one that the medical student had been in such a hurry to dance.

And just as Ivan Ilyich was about to address the bride again, trying this time to tease her with some clever wordplay, the tall officer dashed up and dropped down on one knee with a flourish. She leapt up from the sofa at once and fluttered off with him to join the line for the quadrille. The officer made no attempt to apologize; as for her, she skipped off without a backward glance at the general; in fact she seemed glad to be rid of him.

'Actually, she has every right to do that,' thought Ivan Ilyich. 'And of course they've no idea of manners.'

'Hmm . . . Porfiry, my friend, no need to stand on ceremony,' he said to Pseldonimov. 'You may have . . . things to see to . . . or whatever . . . please, don't mind me.'—'What's he up to, anyway,' he thought, 'is he standing guard over me?'

He was beginning to find Pseldonimov insufferable, with that long neck, and those eyes fixing him so intently. In fact the whole situation was totally unsatisfactory—but Ivan Ilyich couldn't begin to admit this to himself.

*

The quadrille began.

'May I, your Excellency?' asked Akim Petrovich, respectfully proffering the bottle to fill his Excellency's glass.

'I . . . I honestly don't know if . . .'

But Akim Petrovich, his face glowing with reverence, was already pouring the champagne. Having filled the glass, he furtively, almost sneakily, squirming and cringing, poured out a glass for himself; the only difference was that his own had one finger less in it than the other, because that seemed more respectful. Sitting beside his chief, he was suffering like a woman in labour. What could he talk to him about? He had to entertain his Excellency, that was his duty, since he had the honour of keeping him company. Champagne was the solution. And his Excellency was actually pleased to have had his glass filled—not for the sake of the champagne, which was unadulterated warm dishwater, but just . . . morally pleased.

'The old man wants a drink himself,' thought Ivan Ilyich, 'but he doesn't dare have any unless I do. I can't stop him . . . It would be ridiculous for the bottle just to stand between us, untouched.'

He took a sip, and thought it felt better than just sitting there doing nothing.

'I'm here, you know,' he began, pausing as he spoke and stressing his words, 'I'm here, you know, as it were, by accident, and of course it may be . . . that certain people will feel . . . that it's not . . . appropriate for me, to be present at such . . . a celebration.'

Akim Petrovich said nothing, but listened with timid curiosity.

'But I hope you'll understand why I'm here . . . After all, I didn't come here just to drink the wine. Heh-heh!'

Akim Petrovich wanted to give a chuckle himself, just like his Excellency, but somehow it didn't work; once again he couldn't think of anything reassuring to say.

'I'm here . . . in order to, as it were, encourage . . . to demonstrate, as it were, a moral, as it were, purpose,' Ivan Ilyich went on, annoyed with Akim Petrovich for being so dense; but suddenly he stopped short himself. He noticed that poor Akim Petrovich had actually lowered his eyes, as if he was somehow at fault. Feeling embarrassed, the general hastily took another sip, and Akim seized the bottle and topped up his glass as if that was his only hope of salvation.

'You haven't much to say for yourself, have you?' thought Ivan Ilyich, looking sternly at poor Akim Petrovich. The other, feeling those stern eyes of the general's upon him, decided to keep his mouth shut altogether, and not raise his eyes either. And so they sat for a couple of minutes—two very painful minutes for Akim Petrovich.

A word or two about Akim Petrovich. He was a man of the old stamp, as timid as a chicken, brought up to be obsequiously servile, and yet a kind-hearted and even honourable man. He was a Petersburg Russian, meaning that his father, and his father's father, were born, grew up and served in Petersburg and had never once left the city. This is a totally unique type of Russian. Such people have almost no idea of the real Russia, but that doesn't bother them at all. Their whole attention is riveted on Petersburg, and more particularly on their own workplace. All they care about is playing Preference for penny points, the local shop and their monthly wage. They don't know a single Russian custom, nor a single Russian song apart from 'Luchinushka', and that only because the barrel organs play it. You can always tell a Petersburg Russian from a genuine Russian by two essential characteristics. First, no Petersburg Russian, not a single one, ever speaks of *The Petersburg News*: they always call it *The News*. And the second, equally fundamental, is that no Petersburg Russian ever uses the word 'breakfast': they always say '*Frühstück*', with particular stress on the first syllable. These two radical distinguishing marks are infallible. The Petersburg Russian, a humble man, is a type that has gradually developed over the last thirty-five years. Still Akim Petrovich was no fool. If the general had questioned him about anything relevant, he could have replied and sustained a conversation. But it was improper, he felt, for a subordinate even to answer the things Ivan Ilyich was saying—though he was dying of curiosity to find out more details about his Excellency's real intentions . . .

Meantime Ivan Ilyich was becoming more and more pensive, with many thoughts turning over in his head. And every minute he kept absent-mindedly taking another sip from his glass, on and on. Akim Petrovich just as assiduously topped the glass up again. Neither said anything. Ivan Ilyich began watching the dancing, and became intrigued by what he saw. One thing in particular rather surprised him.

The dancing was certainly lively. The guests were dancing in the simplicity of their hearts, wanting to have fun or just have a wild romp. There were very few good dancers, but the bad ones stamped about so vigorously they might have been taken for good dancers too. One who stood out was the officer; he was particularly fond of those figures where he found himself alone, in a sort of solo. Then he would perform the most remarkable bends and twists: standing with his whole body erect as a pole, he would suddenly bend over sideways, so you'd think he was bound to topple over, but then on his next step he'd bend over smartly to the opposite side, at the same acute angle to the floor. His expression remained completely serious; he was absolutely certain that everyone was admiring his dancing. Another dancer, who had filled up on drink before the quadrille even began, dropped fast asleep by his partner's side as early as the second figure, so the lady was left to dance on her own. A young registrar, dancing with the lady in the pale-blue shawl, played the same trick during every figure of each of the five quadrilles danced that evening: falling a little way behind his lady, he seized the end of her shawl, and as they changed partners he managed to press a score of kisses on it while dancing on. His lady, ahead of him, sailed on seemingly quite unaware. The medical student did indeed dance a solo upside down, arousing frantic excitement, stamps and shrieks of delight. Everyone, in fact, was being completely uninhibited. Ivan Ilyich, on whom the wine was now having its effect, was almost smiling, yet a bitter sense of doubt had begun to creep into his soul. Of course, he was very keen on free and easy manners and informality; it was what he wanted, it was what his soul had craved earlier on, when everyone was backing away from him. But now all this informality was really going too far. One lady, for instance, in a dark-blue velvet dress, a worn-out hand-me-down with four previous owners, pinned up her dress during the sixth figure, making it look as if she was wearing pantaloons. This was the very same Kleopatra Semyonovna about whom her partner, the medical student, had said that 'you could try anything on with her'. As for the medical student himself—what could one say? He was another Fokin, no less! How could all this have come about? Earlier on the guests had been backing away, yet now, all of a sudden, they had become so unrestrained! Nothing surprising in that, you might think; but still, what a strange transformation. It must mean something. As if they'd all forgotten there had ever been such a person as Ivan Ilyich. Of course he was the first to laugh, and even ventured to applaud. Akim Petrovich joined in, chuckling respectfully; he himself was obviously happy, and never suspected that his Excellency was beginning to be gnawed by a new worm in his heart.

'You're a splendid dancer, young man,' Ivan Ilyich felt he had to say to the student as he walked past, just after the quadrille was over.

The student whirled round towards him, screwed up his face, bringing it right up close, indecently close, to his Excellency's, and instantly, at the top of his voice, crowed like a cock. That was really too much. Ivan Ilyich got up from the table. But there followed a burst of irrepressible laughter, because the cock's crow had been amazingly lifelike and the grimace completely unexpected. Ivan Ilyich was still standing there in bewilderment when Pseldonimov appeared, bowed and invited him to supper. He was followed by his mother.

'Your Excellency, my dear,' she said with a bow, 'do us the honour, won't you—don't disdain our poor fare.'

'I . . . I really don't know . . .' began Ivan Ilyich, 'I didn't come for that, really . . . I . . . I was just going to leave . . .'

And indeed, he had his hat in his hands. What was more, he had just sworn to himself, at that very moment, that he would leave straight away, no matter what, and not stay longer for anything on earth, and . . . and he stayed. A minute later he was leading the procession to table. Pseldonimov and his mother went ahead to clear the way. He was seated in the place of honour, and another full bottle of champagne appeared by his plate. There were appetizers: salted herrings and vodka. He put out his hand, poured himself a huge glass of vodka, and drank it off. He had never drunk vodka in his life. Now he felt as if he was rolling down a hill, sailing through the air, sailing down and down, that he must catch hold of something to stop himself, but there was nothing he could do.

*

His situation was getting more and more peculiar. By now, fate seemed to be mocking him. God knows what had happened to him over the course of just an hour. When he arrived, he had, as it were, opened his arms to embrace the whole human race and all his subordinates; and now, hardly an hour later, he sensed, he knew with his whole aching heart that he loathed Pseldonimov, and cursed him, and his wife, and his wedding. Worse still—he could see from the man's face, from his very eyes, that Pseldonimov loathed him back; that his look was saying, almost out loud, 'Just go to blazes, damn you! Forcing yourself on us! . .' All this he had already read in the man's eyes some time ago.

Even now, of course, as Ivan Ilyich took his place at table, he would rather have let his hand be cut off than honestly admit, not just aloud but even to himself, that this was actually the case. That moment had not yet come; for now there was still some sort of moral ambivalence. But his heart, his heart . . . how it ached! It begged to be released, to be outside, at rest. He was altogether too kind-hearted, was Ivan Ilyich.

Of course he knew, he knew perfectly well, that he should have left long ago: not just left, but escaped. This wasn't at all what he had been dreaming of, as he stood on the wooden pavement; everything seemed quite different now.

'What did I come for, after all? I didn't come here to eat and drink, did I?' he asked himself as he munched the herring. Bad feelings overwhelmed him; in his heart he ironically criticized his own exploit. He could no longer understand what on earth had made him come.

But how could he leave? To walk out now, without finishing his meal, was unthinkable. 'What'll they say? They'll say I've been seeking out low company. It really will look like that, if I don't stick it out. What'll people say tomorrow, for instance (because everyone will come to hear of it)—Stepan Nikiforovich, for instance, or Semyon Ivanovich, or everyone in the office, or at the Shembels', or the Shubins'? No, when I leave it'll have to be done so that they all understand why I came—my moral aim has to be clear.' But the right moment still wouldn't come. 'They don't even respect me,' he thought; 'what are they laughing at? They're letting themselves go, as if they had no feelings . . . Yes, I've always thought the younger generation has no feelings! No, I've got to stay here at all costs! . . They've just been dancing, but at table they'll all be together . . . I'll talk about some questions, the reforms, Russia's greatness . . . I'll carry them all with me! Yes! Maybe nothing is lost yet . . . Maybe that's how it always happens in real life. But what can I start off with, to get them interested? What plan can I dream up? I'm lost, I'm just lost . . . What is it they want, what do they expect? . . I can see them laughing together there . . . Not laughing at me, are they, for God's sake? But what do I want . . . what am I here for, why aren't I leaving, what am I trying to achieve?' Such were his thoughts, while something like shame—deep, unbearable shame—ripped and tore at his heart.

*

And so it all went on. One thing after another.

Just two minutes after he sat down at table, a terrible thought completely floored him. He suddenly felt that he was dreadfully drunk—not the way he had been earlier, but thoroughly, hopelessly drunk. It was all because of that glass of vodka he had swallowed on top of the champagne; it had had an immediate effect. Now he could feel, he could sense with his whole being, that he was faltering beyond hope of recovery. Of course he had gained a great deal of self-confidence, but his consciousness had not left him, it was screaming at him 'This is bad, it's very bad, it won't do at all!' Of course his tottering, drunken thoughts could never stay fixed on one point for long; he could suddenly feel two opposite sides within himself. Half of him felt self-assured, hungry for victory, determined to brush aside all obstacles, and desperately convinced that he could still win through. The other half made itself felt as an agonizing heartache, as if something was gnawing at his soul. 'What will people say? How will this all end? What will happen tomorrow ... tomorrow ... tomorrow? ..'

Earlier on he had already vaguely sensed that he had enemies among the guests. 'That must be because I was drunk before,' he thought, in anguished doubt. But imagine his horror now, when he saw by unmistakable signs that he really did have enemies at table. There could no longer be any question about it.

'But why? Why?' he thought.

All thirty guests were sitting at table, some of them well stewed. Others, more ominously, were letting themselves go, yelling and shouting at each other, proclaiming toasts before time, flicking bread pellets at the ladies. One unprepossessing individual in a greasy frock coat fell off his chair as soon as he sat down, and remained lying on the floor till the end of dinner. Another was determined to climb onto the table and propose a toast, and it took the officer to control his premature enthusiasm by grabbing hold of his coat-tails. The dinner was a very hotchpotch affair, although a cook had been hired, the serf of some general. There was the galantine, and tongue and potatoes, rissoles with green peas, then a goose and finally the blancmange. To drink there was beer, vodka and sherry. Only the general had a bottle of champagne in front of him; that meant he had to pour it for Akim Petrovich as well as himself, since the man no longer dared do anything on his own initiative. The other guests had to drink the toasts in Georgian wine or whatever came to hand. The table was made up of a number of small tables pushed together—one of them was actually a card table. There were many table-cloths, including one of coloured Yaroslavl cloth. Gentlemen and ladies were seated alternately. Pseldonimov's mother had chosen not to sit at table; she was bustling about organizing things. One sinister female in a reddish silk dress, who had not shown herself earlier, had now turned up; she had a band-aged jaw and an immensely tall cap on her head. This turned out to be the bride's mother, who had eventu-ally consented to emerge from a back room and attend the supper. Up to this point she had kept out of sight, due to her implacable hatred of Pseldonimov's mother; but we shall come back to this. She favoured the general with vicious, even sarcastic looks, and clearly did not want to be presented to him. She struck Ivan Ilyich as extremely suspicious. But others as well as her looked suspicious too, and made him feel fearful and anxious. They all seemed to be united in some conspiracy, directly targeting him. At least that was how it struck him; and for the rest of the supper he became more and more convinced of it. For instance: there was a gentleman with a little beard, some kind of freelance artist, who was especially malevolent; he actually looked at Ivan Ilyich several times, and then turned to his neighbour and whispered something. Another man, a student, was admittedly quite drunk by now, but even so, several things about him were suspicious. The medical student, too, was far from reassuring. Even the officer was not quite trustworthy. But the journalist on *The Firebrand* was the worst, sprawling on his chair and blazing with violent, unconcealed hatred; he had such a proud, arrogant expression, and he snorted so provocatively! And although none of the other guests took any particular notice of this journalist, who had only become a liberal by contributing four little poems to *The Firebrand*—although, indeed, they apparently disliked him—even so, when a bread pellet suddenly landed close to Ivan Ilyich, obviously aimed at him, he would have staked his head that the culprit was none other than the journalist on *The Firebrand*.

All this, of course, had a lamentable effect on him.

Ivan Ilyich noticed another particularly unpleasant thing. He became convinced that he was beginning to pronounce his words thickly and laboriously; that he wanted to say a great deal, but his tongue wouldn't obey him. And then he felt that he was beginning to forget what he was saying, and most importantly, was uttering explosive snorts and giggles, though there was nothing whatever to laugh about. This state of mind soon passed, after a glass of champagne which Ivan Ilyich had in fact poured himself earlier, but had never meant to drink. He had knocked it back more or less by accident, after which he suddenly felt weepy. He could sense himself falling into a most peculiar, maudlin mood: all at once he began to love them, love them all, even Pseldonimov, even the journalist on *The Firebrand*. He wanted to hug them all, forget everything and make his peace with them. And more: he wanted to tell them everything, open-heartedly, everything— what a kind, good man he was, and how amazingly talented; how nobly he was going to serve his country, how good he was at entertaining the ladies, and above all, how progressive he was, how humanely he was ready to condescend to everybody, even the lowest of the low; and finally, in conclusion, to explain in all sincerity the reasons that had led him to present himself uninvited at Pseldonimov's house, drink off two bottles of his champagne, and delight him by his presence.

'The truth, above all! Open-hearted truth! I'll win them over by my open-heartedness. They will believe me—I can see that clearly. Although they're giving me hostile looks, once I explain everything to them, I'll win them over completely. They'll fill their glasses and drink my health with enthusiastic shouts. The officer, I'm sure, will smash his glass against his spurs. They may even shout 'Hurrah!' Even if they decide to toss me in the air, the way hussars do—I wouldn't resist, in fact it might be a very good thing. I'll kiss the bride on her brow, she's a sweet girl. Akim Petrovich is an excellent chap too. Pseldonimov, of course, will improve with time. He needs more social polish, as it were . . . And although this whole younger generation of course lacks that delicacy of soul . . . even so, I'll explain to them about Russia's destiny today, as one of the great European powers. And I'll mention the peasant question too, and . . . and they'll all love me, and I'll come out of it triumphant! . .'

Of course these dreams were very pleasant ones, but the unpleasant thing was that in the midst of all his rosy hopes Ivan Ilyich suddenly became aware of possessing another unexpected talent, namely spitting. Or at least, spittle had suddenly begun to spray out of his mouth whether he wanted it to or not. He first noticed this on Akim Petrovich, whose cheek he had spattered, and who was now sitting there not daring to wipe it off, out of a sense of respect. Ivan Ilyich picked up his napkin and wiped him clean himself. But this action at once struck him as so absurd, so completely out of order, that he stopped talking and began to wonder. Though Akim drank off his glass, he still sat there as if he had been scalded. Ivan Ilyich realized that he had just spent almost a quarter of an hour telling him about something intensely interesting, but that Akim Petrovich had not only looked embarrassed as he listened, but actually seemed frightened. Pseldonimov, sitting one place further off, was also craning his neck towards him and bending his head to one side to listen to him, with a most disagreeable expression. He actually seemed to be keeping an eye on him. Looking over all the guests, Ivan Ilyich could see many of them looking straight at him and laughing. But the strangest thing of all was that this did not in the least put him off his stride; he now took another gulp from his glass and addressed the whole company.

'I was saying just now,' he began, at the top of his voice, 'I was saying just now to Akim Petrovich, ladies and gentlemen, that Russia . . . yes, Russia, I mean . . . in short, you understand what I'm trying to say . . . Russia, I am profoundly convinced, is passing through . . . a period of hu-humanity . . .'

'Hu-humanity!' came an echo from the far end of the table.

'Hu-hu!'

'Toot-toot!'

Ivan Ilyich tailed off. Pseldonimov got up from his chair and looked round to see who had shouted. Akim Petrovich furtively shook his head, as if to admonish the company. Ivan Ilyich noticed him quite clearly, felt excruciatingly embarrassed but said nothing.

'Humanity!' he went on stubbornly, 'And only a short while back I was saying to Stepan Niki-ki-forovich . . . yes . . . that . . . that the renewal, as it were, of things—'

'Your Excellency!' came a loud voice from the far end of the table.

'What can I do for you?'

'Nothing whatever, your Excellency, I got carried away, pray continue! Pra-a-ay continue!' the voice repeated. Ivan Ilyich winced.

'The renewal, so to speak, of these very things—'

'Your Excellency!' the voice called out again.

'What is it?'

'Hello there!'

Ivan Ilyich could control himself no longer. He broke off and turned to the insulting individual who was disturbing the peace. He was a very young student who had already drunk a great deal, and aroused the greatest suspicion in Ivan Ilyich. He had been shouting for some time, and had smashed a glass and two plates, insisting that this was what had to happen at a wedding. When Ivan Ilyich turned to him, the officer was just beginning to give the noisy lad a stern talking-to.

'What's up, what are you yelling for? We ought to throw you out, that's what!'

'It's not about you, your Excellency, not about you! Do go on!' shouted the irrepressible schoolboy, sprawling over his chair. 'Do go on, I'm listening, I'm very, ve-ry pleased with you! Admir-able, admir-able!'

'Drunken brat!' whispered Pseldonimov.

'I can see he's drunk, but . . .'

'It's just that I was telling a very amusing story, your Excellency!' began the officer. 'It was about a lieutenant in our unit, who used to talk to his senior officers in the same way; so now the lad's imitating him.

Whatever his commanding officer said, he'd keep answering "admir-able, admir-able!" He was dismissed from the service for that, a full ten years ago.'

'Who was this lieutenant?'

'One of our unit, your Excellency, he went crazy over the word "admirable". First they treated him gently, then they locked him up . . . The commanding officer talked to him like a father, but the young man answered back—"admir-able, admir-able!" The strange thing was, he was a brave officer, all of six foot tall. They wanted to court-martial him, but then they saw he was crazy.'

'So . . . a schoolboy. Schoolboy behaviour could be treated less severely . . . Myself, I'd have been prepared to let him off . . .'

'There was a medical report, your Excellency.'

'What! They did an autopsy?'

'Not at all, he was perfectly alive, sir.'

A burst of loud laughter broke out, in which almost everyone joined, though up till then they had been showing restraint. Ivan Ilyich was furious.

'Gentlemen, gentlemen!' he shouted, barely stammering at first. 'I'm perfectly capable of realizing that a living man wouldn't be autopsied. I had just supposed that in his madness he had been no longer alive . . . that is, had died . . . what I mean to say is . . . you don't love me . . . But I love you all . . . yes, and I love Por . . . Porfiry . . . I'm lowering myself, speaking to you like this . . .'

At that moment a gigantic gob of spittle flew out of Ivan Ilyich's mouth and splattered over the tablecloth, in a most conspicuous place. Pseldonimov hurled himself forward to wipe it off with a napkin. This latest catastrophe completely crushed Ivan Ilyich.

'Gentlemen, this is too much!' he cried in despair.

'The man's drunk, your Excellency,' Pseldonimov whispered again.

'Porfiry! I can see that you're . . . all . . . yes! I hope, I say . . . yes, I call on everyone to tell me: how have I lowered myself?'

Ivan Ilyich was on the verge of tears.

'Your Excellency, please!'

'Porfiry, I put it to you . . . Listen, if I came . . . yes . . . yes, to this wedding, I had a purpose. I wanted to morally elevate . . . I wanted people to feel. Now I ask you all: am I deeply humiliated in your eyes, or not?'

A sepulchral silence. That was just it—a sepulchral silence, to such a straightforward question. 'What harm would it do them, just to give me a shout, right now?'—the thought flashed through his Excellency's mind. But the guests only exchanged glances. Akim

Petrovich was sitting there more dead than alive, while Pseldonimov, numb with terror, was repeating to himself the dreadful question which had occurred to him a long time before:

'What'll I get for all this tomorrow?'

Suddenly the journalist from *The Firebrand*, who was very drunk by now but had so far been sitting in morose silence, addressed himself directly to Ivan Ilyich. With glittering eyes, he answered him in the name of the whole company.

'Yes sir!' he thundered, 'yes, sir, you have humiliated yourself, yes, you're a reactionary! A re-act-ion-ary!'

'Young man, you forget yourself! Who do you think you're, I mean, talking to?' cried Ivan Ilyich in a rage, jumping up from his seat again.

'I'm talking to you, and secondly I'm not a young man ... You've come here to put on airs and curry favour.'

'Pseldonimov, what's going on!' Ivan Ilyich cried.

But Pseldonimov had also jumped up from his seat, in such a state of horror that he froze to the spot and had no idea what to do next. The guests, too, were sitting dumbly in their places. The artist and the schoolboy, however, were clapping and shouting 'Bravo, bravo!'

The journalist continued to yell with irrepressible fury: 'Yes, you came here to show off how humane you are! You spoilt the party for everyone. You drank champagne without thinking that it's more than a clerk on ten roubles a month can afford. And I bet you're one of those bosses with an eye for the pretty young wives of your staff! And that's not all—I'm sure you're a supporter of state monopolies ... Yes, yes, yes!'

'Pseldonimov! Pseldonimov!' cried Ivan Ilyich, stretching out his hands to him. He felt every one of the journalist's words as a fresh dagger to his heart.

'Directly, your Excellency, don't trouble yourself!' cried Pseldonimov with determination. He ran over to the journalist, seized him by the collar and dragged him away from the table. One could never have expected the weedy Pseldonimov to show such physical strength. But the journalist was very drunk, and Pseldonimov perfectly sober. He gave the man two or three punches in the back and shoved him out of the room.

'Villains, all of you!' yelled the journalist. 'I'll lampoon the lot of you in tomorrow's *Firebrand*!'

Everyone leapt up.

'Your Excellency, your Excellency!' cried Pseldonimov, his mother and various guests, milling around the general, 'Your Excellency, please don't worry!'

'No, no,' cried the general, 'I am destroyed . . . I came to . . . I wanted to bless you, so to speak. And see what I get, for all . . . all that I . . .'

He sank down on a chair looking barely conscious, laid both hands on the table and bowed his head over them, straight into a plate of blancmange. No need to describe the general horror. After a minute he stood up, evidently trying to leave; but he staggered, tripped against a chair leg, crashed full tilt onto the floor and began to snore . . .

This happens to non-drinkers, when they accidentally get drunk. They remain conscious to the last, to the very last moment, and then fall as if felled by a blow. Ivan Ilyich lay on the floor, deeply unconscious. Pseldonimov thrust his hands in his hair and froze in that attitude. The guests began hastily dispersing, each discussing the events from his own point of view. It was almost three in the morning.

*

The real trouble was that Pseldonimov's circumstances were far worse than could have been imagined, however unappealing his situation must have seemed just then. And now, as Ivan Ilyich lies on the floor and Pseldonimov stands over him tearing his hair in despair, let us interrupt the flow of this story to give a few words of explanation about Porfiry Petrovich Pseldonimov himself.

No more than a month before his wedding, he had been living in a state of abject poverty. He came from one of the provinces where his father had at some time or other been in service in some department or other, and died while awaiting trial on some charge. Pseldonimov spent a whole year living in utter misery in Petersburg until, five months before his wedding, he got his ten-rouble job. That revived him in body and spirit, but circumstances soon crushed him again. There were then only two Pseldonimovs left in the whole world, himself and his mother, who had left the provinces after her husband's death. Mother and son lived in misery together, starving in the freezing cold and eating dubious foods. There were days when Pseldonimov had to go down to the Fontanka River for a jug of water to drink on the spot. When he got his job, he managed to settle himself and his mother in one corner or another of various people's flats. She began taking in washing, while he spent four or five months scrimping and saving to get himself a pair of boots and some sort of overcoat. And what a hard time he had in the office! His bosses would stop by to ask him how long it was since he'd been to the bathhouse. There were rumours that colonies of bedbugs had set up their nests inside his uniform collar.

But Pseldonimov was tough. On the surface, he was meek and mild; he had only the most basic education, and was almost never heard to speak a word. I am not certain whether he ever thought about things, made plans, indulged in theories, or had dreams of any kind. But he did develop a sort of instinctive, obstinate, unconscious determination to fight his way out of his bad situation. He had the stubbornness of an ant. If you destroy an ants' nest, they'll begin rebuilding it straight away; destroy it again, and they'll start rebuilding again, and so on, tirelessly. He was a constructive, domestic thing. You could see written on his brow that he would make his way, build his nest, and maybe even put something aside. His mother was the only person in the world who loved him, and she loved him beyond anything. She was a firm, hard-working, tireless woman, but kind-hearted too. They might have gone on living in those corners of rented rooms for another five or six years, perhaps—until their situation improved—if they had not met the retired Titular Councillor Mlekopitaev, who had been a treasurer in some provincial office, but had recently moved to Petersburg and settled there with his family.

He knew Pseldonimov, and had once been under an obligation to his father. He had some money, not much of course, but he did have some; how much exactly, no one knew—neither his wife, nor his elder daughter, nor the relatives. He had two daughters, and as he was a dreadful bully, a drunkard and a domestic tyrant, not to mention an invalid, he suddenly hit upon the idea of marrying off one of his daughters to Pseldonimov. 'I know him,' he said, 'his father was a good man, and the son will be a good man too.' Whatever Mlekopitaev wanted, he got, and whatever he said was done.

He was a very strange sort of bully. He spent most of his time sitting in an armchair, having lost the use of his legs through some illness—however, it didn't stop him drinking vodka. He would drink and swear for days on end. He was a spiteful man, always needing a victim to torment. He kept a number of female relations living with him for that purpose—his own sister, a sickly, quarrelsome woman; two sisters of his wife's, also ill-natured gossip-mongers; and his old aunt, who had happened to break one of her ribs in an accident. He also had another dependant in his home, a Russianized German woman whom he kept with him because of her talent for telling him stories from the *Arabian Nights*. His only pleasure lay in mocking all these wretched hangers-on, swearing at them till the air turned blue, although none of them, not even his wife (who had been born with the toothache) dared to venture a word in his presence. He set them at each other's throats, inventing and stirring up gossip and spite among them, and then guffawed with delight when he saw them on the point of tearing each other's eyes out. He was delighted when his elder daughter, who had married and spent ten years living in poverty with her officer husband, eventually became a widow and moved back to his home with her three small, sickly children. He loathed the children, but as their arrival provided more material for his daily experiments, the old man was very happy. This whole brood of ill-natured women and sickly children and their tormentor were crowded into a wooden house on the Petersburg Side, where they went hungry because the old man was close-fisted and only handed out his money a kopek at a time, though keeping himself well supplied with vodka; they went short of sleep because the old man suffered from insomnia and demanded to be entertained. In short, they were all poor and miserable, and cursed their fate.

It was at this point that Mlekopitaev's eye fell on Pseldonimov. He was impressed by the young man's long nose and meek looks. His own plain and weakly younger daughter had just turned seventeen. Although she had spent some time attending a German *Schule*, she had come away with little more than her ABC. After that she grew up, skinny and scrofulous, in dread of her crippled, drunken father's crutch, in that hotbed of domestic tale-telling, eavesdropping and gossip. She had never had any friends, nor any common sense. She had long wanted to get married. In company she was tongue-tied, but at home with her mother and the other women she was spiteful and crotchety. She particularly enjoyed pinching and smacking her sister's children, and telling tales on them for pilfering sugar or bread; this gave rise to endless unforgiving quarrels between her and her elder sister. The old man had himself offered her to Pseldonimov. Poor though he was, the young man still asked for time to think it over. He and his mother hesitated over it a long time. But the bride was to bring a house as her dowry—a wooden one, true, and a nasty, single-storey one, but still worth something. And four hundred roubles, too: how long would it have taken them to save that up? 'Why am I taking a man into my home?' yelled the drunken bully. 'Firstly, because you're all women, and I'm bored with nothing but women about me. I want Pseldonimov to dance to my tune too, because I'm his benefactor. And secondly, I'm doing it because you're all fed up and don't want me to; so I'll do it to spite you. I've said it and I'll do it! And you, little Porfiry, make sure you beat her once you're married: she's had seven devils living in her ever since she was born. You drive them all out—I'll get the stick ready . . .'

Pseldonimov said nothing, but he had already made his mind up. He and his mother were moved over to the house before the wedding, cleaned up, and provided with clothes, shoes and money for the occasion. The old man took them under his wing, perhaps just because the rest of the family resented them. He even took a liking to the mother, old Pseldonimova, and avoided making fun of her. But a week before the wedding he did force Pseldonimov to do a Cossack dance for him. 'All right, that'll do, I just wanted to make sure you don't forget yourself in my presence,' he said when the dance was over. The funds he supplied for the wedding were just adequate, with nothing to spare, and he invited all his own friends and relations. On Pseldonimov's side there was no one but the journalist on *The Firebrand* and Akim Petrovich, the guest of honour. Pseldonimov was well aware that his bride was revolted by him and would much rather have had the officer. But he bore everything patiently: that was what he had agreed with his mother. The old man had spent the whole of the wedding day drunk, scattering foul-mouthed insults, while the entire family took refuge in the back rooms, cowering together amid a stifling stench. The front rooms were set aside for the dance and supper. Eventually, around eleven at night, the old man at last fell into a drunken slumber; the bride's mother, who had been particularly annoyed with Pseldonimov's mother that day, then decided to forget her grudge and come out to attend the dance and the supper. The arrival of Ivan Ilyich had turned everything upside down. Mlekopitaeva was mortified, took offence and complained that she had never been warned that an actual general was invited. They assured her that he had come uninvited, but she was too stupid to believe it. Champagne was needed. Pseldonimov's mother turned out to have just one rouble, while Pseldonimov himself had not a single kopek. They had to go and grovel to spiteful old Mlekopitaeva, begging her for money to buy one bottle, and then a second. They painted a glowing picture of Pseldonimov's future in the service, and his career, and pleaded for all they were worth. She finally handed over some of her own money, but forced Pseldonimov to drain such a cup of acrimony and bile that he kept running to the little room containing the marriage bed, silently clutching his hair, trembling with impotent rage, and flinging himself head first onto the bed destined for the joys of paradise. Oh, yes!

Ivan Ilyich had no idea of the cost of those two bottles of Jacquesson's champagne he had drunk off that evening. So imagine Pseldonimov's horror, anguish and despair when Ivan Ilyich's visit culminated in this unexpected way. He could see no end of fuss, perhaps a whole night of shrieks and tears from the cantankerous bride, and hard words from her half-witted family. He already had a headache, he already had a dark mist before his eyes—and now Ivan Ilyich needed help, they had to get hold of a doctor at three in the morning, or a carriage to take him home, and a carriage it had to be, because they couldn't possibly hand over such a personage to an ordinary cab driver to drive him home in his present condition. And where could they find the money to pay for a carriage? The bride's mother, furious with the general for not having spoken a word to her at supper, or even looked at her, declared that she didn't have another kopek. Perhaps she really didn't. So where could he find the money? What was he to do? Yes indeed, he had good reason to tear his hair.

*

Meanwhile Ivan Ilyich had been carried over to a little leather sofa in the dining room. The tables were being cleared and put back in their places. Pseldonimov was haring about in all directions trying to borrow money—he even tried to get the servants to lend him some, but no one had any. Then he actually ventured to trouble Akim Petrovich, who had stayed on longer than the others. But he, though a kind-hearted man, became so bewildered and frightened the moment he heard money mentioned that he talked the most unexpected nonsense.

'Another time, with pleasure,' he muttered; 'but right now . . . truly, you'll have to excuse me . . .'

And picking up his hat, he ran out of the house as fast as he could go. Only the good-natured youth who had been talking about the dream book now turned out to be any use, and even that was a waste of time. He too had stayed behind when the others left, feeling really sorry for Pseldonimov's troubles. Pseldonimov, his mother and the youth had talked things over and finally decided not to send for a doctor, but to find a carriage to take the sick man home, and meanwhile try a variety of home remedies such as wetting his head and temples with cold water, putting ice on the top of his head, and the like, until the carriage arrived. Pseldonimov's mother set about applying these remedies, while the youth ran off to find a carriage. Since there wasn't even a single common cab to be found on the Petersburg Side at that hour, he set out for some stables a long way off, to wake the coachmen there.

They started haggling; the coachmen insisted that even five roubles wasn't enough for a carriage at that time of night, but eventually they settled for three. But at four in the morning, when the young man arrived with the hired carriage, the plans had long ago been changed. It turned out that Ivan Ilyich, still unconscious, was so sick, groaning and thrashing about, that moving him and driving him off in his present state was quite impossible and even dangerous. 'What will happen next?' wondered Pseldonimov, in the depths of despair. What was to be done? And that led to another problem. If the sick man was to be kept in the house, where should they take him? And where lay him down? There were only two beds in the whole house: one enormous double bed used by old Mlekopitaev and his wife, and another double one in imitation walnut, just bought for the newlyweds. The other inhabitants, all those women, slept side by side on the floor, mostly on worn-out, stinking feather beds, quite unpresentable. And there were only just enough of those, or not even. So where to put the sick man? True, they might still have rustled up a quilt—pulled it out from under one of the sleepers, even—but where to lay it? It turned out that it would have to be spread in the parlour, which was furthest from the heart of the family and had its own door to the outside. But what to lay it on? Surely not on chairs? We know that beds can be made up on chairs, but that only happens with schoolchildren home for the weekend. Doing the same thing for Ivan Ilyich would be disrespectful. What would he say next morning, if he woke up to find himself on a row of chairs? Pseldonimov wouldn't hear of anything of the sort. There was only one way out: to carry him to the bridal bed. This bridal bed, as we have said, stood in the little room next to the dining room. It had a double mattress, just bought and never used, clean linen and four pillows in pink calico covered in frilly muslin pillowcases. The blanket was of pink satin with a quilted pattern. Muslin curtains hung down from a golden ring over the bed. So everything was just as it should be, and almost all the guests had visited the bedroom and admired the décor. The bride, although she couldn't stand Pseldonimov, had crept in several times that evening on the sly to take a look. Imagine her furious outrage when she heard that a sick man, suffering from some kind of cholera, was going to be brought in and laid on her nuptial bed! The bride's mother spoke up for her, sounding off and threatening to complain to her husband in the morning. But Pseldonimov showed what he was made of, and stood his ground: Ivan Ilyich was carried in, and a bed for the newlyweds was made up on chairs in the parlour. The bride started whingeing and getting ready to pinch everyone, but didn't dare disobey—she was no stranger to her papa's crutch, and she knew he would be bound to demand a full explanation next day. To pacify her, the pink quilt and the four pillows in their muslin pillowcases were brought into the big room too. That was the moment when the youth reappeared with the carriage. When he discovered that it was no longer needed, he was dreadfully frightened. It turned out that he would have to pay himself, and he had never owned so much as ten kopeks in his life. Pseldonimov declared himself completely penniless. They tried arguing with the driver, but he kicked up a rumpus and banged on the shutters. How the whole thing ended, I'm not quite sure. I believe the youth was held hostage and carried off to Peski, to Fourth Rozhdestvensky Street, where he hoped to wake a student spending the night with friends, and see if he had any money. It was past four o'clock before the young couple were left alone, locked up in the parlour. Pseldonimov's mother spent the whole night by the sick man's bedside. She settled down on a rug on the floor and covered herself with an overcoat, but got no sleep because she had to get up every few minutes. Ivan Ilyich had developed terrible stomach trouble. Pseldonimova, a brave and big-hearted woman, undressed him herself, got all his clothes off him, looked after him as if he were her own son, and spent all night carrying vital pots and basins out to the corridor and back again. But the night's disasters were far from over.

*

No more than ten minutes after the young couple were shut up alone in the parlour, ear-piercing screams were suddenly heard from there: not cries of joy, but screams of the most sinister kind. The screams were followed by a loud noise, a crash as of chairs falling over—and a whole bevy of women, arrayed in every kind of déshabillé and gasping with alarm, burst into the room, which was still dark. There was the bride's mother, her elder sister (who had left her sickly children behind for the moment), and her three aunts (including the one with the fractured rib). Even the cook turned up; and even the German hanger-on who told stories (she had had her own personal feather bed dragged bodily from under her for the newlyweds—it was the best in the house, and represented her entire property). All these respectable and keen-eyed women had tiptoed out of the kitchen and across the corridor a full quarter of an hour before, to eavesdrop in the anteroom, devoured by the most inexplicable curiosity. By now someone had quickly lit a candle, revealing to all an unexpected sight. The chairs, which had only been supporting the broad feather bed at its edges, had slid apart under the double weight of its occupants, and the feather bed had slipped to the floor between them. The young bride was sobbing with rage. This time she was mortally offended. There stood Pseldonimov, morally destroyed, looking like a criminal caught in the act. He made no attempt to stick up for himself. Gasps and shrieks came from all sides. Pseldonimov's mother arrived too, but on this occasion the bride's mamma carried the day hands down. She began by showering Pseldonimov with strange and mostly undeserved reproaches along the lines of 'What sort of a husband are you anyway, to let this happen? What use are you, boy, after a disgrace like this?' and the like; after which she took her daughter's hand and led her away from her husband and into her own room, making herself personally responsible for facing the ferocious father's angry questions next day. All the others followed her out of the room, sighing and shaking their heads. Pseldonimov was left alone with his mother. She tried to comfort him, but he sent her out at once.

Nothing could comfort him. He found his way to the sofa and sat down to reflect morosely on what had happened, barefoot and in his nightshirt. His thoughts whirled this way and that. From time to time, almost mechanically, he looked round this room where a short while ago the dancers had been spinning wildly about, and where cigarette smoke still lingered in the air. Cigarette ends and sweet papers lay scattered among the puddles on the dirty floor. The wreck of the bridal couch and the upset chairs bore witness to the transience of man's best and surest earthly hopes and dreams. He sat there for almost an hour, thinking the darkest thoughts. For example: what would happen to him at work? He was agonizingly aware that he would have to change his job at all costs; staying put was impossible, because of what had happened that evening. And he thought of Mlekopitaev, who would no doubt make him do another Cossack dance next day, to make sure he was still submissive enough. And he realized that although Mlekopitaev had paid fifty roubles for the wedding, every kopek of which had been spent, he hadn't yet dreamt of handing over the four-hundred-rouble dowry—it hadn't even been mentioned. Indeed, even the house hadn't yet been formally made over to him. Then he thought about his wife, who had deserted him at the most critical moment in his life, and about the tall officer who had got down on one knee before her. He had already noticed that; and he thought of the seven devils which possessed her, as witnessed by her very own father, and of the stick waiting to drive them out . . . Of course he felt confident he could put up with a great deal; but destiny was dealing him such shocks that he might end up doubting his own strength to bear them.

Such were Pseldonimov's miserable thoughts. Meanwhile the candle end was burning down; its flickering light, falling directly onto Pseldonimov's profile, cast a colossal shadow on the wall, with his neck stretched out, his hooked nose and two wisps of hair sticking up from his forehead and the back of his head. Eventually, as the cool morning air blew in, he stood up, chilled to the bone and numb to his soul, found his way to the feather bed lying on the floor between the chairs, and without rearranging anything, nor snuffing out the candle end, nor even laying a pillow under his head, he crawled on all fours onto the feather bed and fell into a deadly, leaden sleep, like a man condemned to be publicly flogged next day.

*

But then, what could compare with that anguished night spent by Ivan Ilyich Pralinsky on wretched Pseldonimov's nuptial bed? For quite a time he suffered agonies of headache, vomiting and other sorts of highly disagreeable attacks which gave him not a moment's peace. The torments were infernal. The moments of faint consciousness that illuminated his brain revealed such an abyss of horror, such dark and revolting images, that he had better not have regained consciousness at all. His head was still in a chaotic jumble. For instance, he recognized Pseldonimov's mother, he heard her gentle and harmless exhortations: 'put up with it, my dear, put up with it, love, you'll be better soon,' but though he recognized her, he couldn't find any logical reason for her being there. He was troubled by revolting visions: most of the time he thought he saw Semyon Ivanovich, but on a closer look he realized that this wasn't Semyon Ivanovich at all but Pseldonimov's nose. Other figures also flashed before him: the freelance artist, the officer, the old woman with the bandaged jaw. What intrigued him most was the golden ring suspended above his head, with the curtains threaded through it. He could clearly make it out by the dim light of the candle end that lit the room, and he kept wondering—what was the point of that ring, why was it there, and what could it mean? He asked the old woman about it several times, but probably didn't get the words out right, and the old woman evidently didn't understand him, despite his best efforts. Finally, towards morning, his attacks of illness passed off and he fell into a deep and dreamless sleep. He slept for about an hour, and woke almost fully conscious but with an unbearable headache. His tongue felt as if it had been turned into a cloth rag, and his whole mouth was filled with a revolting taste. He sat up in bed, looked round and started thinking. The pale light of dawn, peeping through the cracks of the shutters, cast a narrow strip of shimmering light on the opposite wall. It was about seven o'clock. But when Ivan Ilyich suddenly realized and remembered what had happened to him last evening; when he recalled all his adventures at supper, the failure of his noble enterprise, and his speech at table; when he saw in an instant, with horrifying clarity, all the possible consequences, everything that people would now say about him, and think about him; when he looked round the room and at last saw the hideous, sorry state to which he had reduced his clerk's peaceable bridal couch—oh, then his heart was overwhelmed with such deadly shame and torment that he cried out aloud, hid his face in his hands and flung himself back on the pillow in despair. A minute later he leapt up from the bed and saw his clothes on the chair beside it, neatly brushed and folded. Grabbing them in frantic haste, looking around in vague terror, he pulled them on as quickly as he could. There on another chair was his overcoat, and his fur cap with his yellow gloves inside it. He meant to slink away unnoticed. But the door

opened and old Pseldonimova came in with an earthenware jug and basin, carrying a towel over her shoulder. She set the jug down and declared without further
ado that he had absolutely got to wash.

'Come on, dearie, have a wash, you can't go without washing . . .'

In that instant Ivan Ilyich realized that if there was
a single being in the whole world of whom he need not
be afraid, one person before whom he need not be
ashamed, it was that old lady. He washed himself. And
long afterwards, at painful moments in his life, he
remembered—among other pangs of conscience—
the scene of that awakening, and the earthenware
basin and the china jug filled with cold water with
pieces of ice still floating in it, and the oval cake of
soap in its pink wrapper with embossed lettering—
fifteen kopeks' worth of soap, evidently bought for the
newlyweds but now to be first unwrapped and used by
Ivan Ilyich, and the old lady with the damask towel
over her left shoulder. The cold water refreshed him;
he dried himself, and without addressing a word to his
sister of mercy, without even thanking her, he grabbed
his cap, snatched his coat from Pseldonimova's hands,
flung it over his shoulders, rushed across the corridor,
through the kitchen (where the cat was already
mewing, and the cook was sitting up in bed full of avid

curiosity to watch him go), ran out through the yard and into the street, and hurled himself into a passing cab. It was a frosty morning, with an icy, yellowish fog still hiding the houses and everything else. Ivan Ilyich turned up his collar. He felt that everyone was watching him, everyone recognized him, everything would be found out . . .

*

For eight days he stayed at home and never showed himself at the office. He was ill, agonizingly ill, but it was a moral ailment rather than a physical one. Over those eight days he lived through perfect hell; no doubt those days were credited to him in the next world. There were minutes when he contemplated becoming a monk. Yes, there really were. His imagination ranged far and wide. He pictured gentle singing from under the ground, an open coffin, life in a solitary cell, forests, caves; but as soon as he came to himself again, he realized that all this was the most dreadful nonsense and exaggeration, and grew ashamed of it. Then he started having attacks of moral doubt, centred on his *existence manquée*. Shame would blaze up in his soul once more, overwhelming him in an instant, consuming him and reopening his wounds. He shuddered as he imagined a variety of scenes. What would people say about him, what would they think about him; how would he walk into his office; what whispers would dog him for a whole year, or ten years, or all his life? His story would go down to posterity. Sometimes he felt so faint-hearted he could even have driven straight to Semyon Ivanovich to beg for his forgiveness and friendship. He made no attempt to justify himself, but roundly condemned himself; he could find no justification, and was ashamed even to try.

He also thought of resigning his post at once, and leading a solitary life devoted to the happiness of the human race. Whatever happened, he would have to change his whole circle of acquaintances, so thoroughly that no one should remember anything about him. Then he started thinking that this was rubbish too, and that if he became stricter with his subordinates, the situation could still be saved. That made him feel more hopeful and confident. Finally, after a full eight days of doubt and anguish, he could bear the uncertainty no longer, and *un beau matin* he made up his mind to set out for the office.

Earlier on, sitting miserably at home, he had pictured to himself a thousand times what would happen when he walked into his office. He felt horribly certain that he would hear duplicitous whispers behind his back, see duplicitous faces around him, detect the most malignant smiles. But what was his amazement when nothing of the sort happened! He was greeted respectfully; people bowed to him; everyone was grave; everyone was busy. As he made his way to his own room, his heart was filled with joy.

He got down to work at once, taking it very seriously; listened to reports and explanations, and took decisions. Never in his life, he felt, had he reasoned so intelligently or decided matters so judiciously as that morning. He could see that people were pleased with him, and honoured him, and treated him with respect. Not even the most sensitive, insecure person could have found anything to object to. Everything was going splendidly.

Eventually Akim Petrovich appeared with some papers. As he walked in, something seemed to stab at Ivan Ilyich's heart—but only for an instant. He got down to business with Akim Petrovich, spoke with dignity, pointed out what needed to be done, gave explanations. All he was aware of was that he avoided looking too long at Akim Petrovich—or rather, Akim Petrovich seemed afraid to look at him. But now Akim Petrovich had finished, and was gathering up his papers.

'And there's another request,' Akim Petrovich added as neutrally as he could; 'the clerk Pseldonimov has applied for a transfer to another department . . .

his Excellency Semyon Ivanovich Shipulenko promised him a position there. He requests your kind support, your Excellency.'

'Ah, so he's transferring,' said Ivan Ilyich, feeling a colossal weight being lifted from his heart. He glanced at Akim Petrovich, and at that moment their eyes met.

'Certainly, for my part, I'll . . . I'll use . . . I'm willing.'

Akim Petrovich was clearly anxious to slip away as quickly as he could. But suddenly, in a rush of noble feeling, Ivan Ilyich made up his mind to speak out. Once again, he was filled with inspiration.

'Tell him,' he began, directing a candid, deeply meaningful look at Akim Petrovich, 'tell Pseldonimov that I wish him no ill; no, not the least ill! . . On the contrary, I am even prepared to forget all that has passed, to forget it all, all of it . . .'

But he broke off abruptly, to stare in astonishment at Akim Petrovich's strange reaction. For some reason, the man had suddenly changed from a rational human being into a complete halfwit. Instead of listening and hearing him out, he had started blushing in the stupidest way, making almost indecently hasty little bows, one after another, and backing towards the door. His whole attitude made it clear that he was longing to vanish through the floor, or rather to get back to his own desk as quickly as possible. Left on his own, Ivan Ilyich got up from his chair in confusion, and stared into the mirror without noticing his own face.

'No: strictness, nothing but strictness, strictness!' he whispered to himself almost unconsciously. Suddenly his whole face flushed deep crimson. He was filled with such shame and distress as he had never experienced in the most unbearable moments of his eight days' illness.

'I didn't hold out!' he said to himself, sinking helplessly onto his chair.

CONVERSATIONS IN A GRAVEYARD

(Bobok)

SEMYON ARDALYONOVICH ASKED me the other day: 'Ivan Ivanovich, are you ever going to be sober, for goodness' sake?'

An odd question. I'm a timid man, I don't take offence—but look, now they're passing me off as a lunatic. An artist once happened to paint my portrait; 'After all,' he says, 'you're a writer, aren't you?' So I let him do it, and he exhibited it. And then I read: 'Go and look at this morbid, half-mad face.'

That may be so—but how can you put it straight into print? What gets printed should be dignified, there should be ideals, but here . . .

At least put it a bit indirectly; that's what style is for. But no, he doesn't want anything indirect. Humour and proper style are going out of fashion these days;

abuse is replacing wit. I don't take offence: I'm not such a great writer, I won't go mad over it. I wrote a story, and it didn't get printed. Wrote a pamphlet—it was turned down. I touted those pamphlets round a lot of editorial offices, and they were all turned down. 'There's no salt in them,' they said.

'What kind of salt would you like,' I asked sarcastically; 'Attic salt?'

He didn't even get the point. Mostly I do translations for booksellers, from French. And I write advertisements targeted at merchants. 'A rarity!' I say. 'Red tea from our own plantations . . .' I wrote a panegyric on his Excellency the late Piotr Matveyevich which earned me quite a packet. I did a compilation called *The Art of Pleasing the Ladies* for one bookseller. Well, I've done about six little books like that in my life. I'd like to put together a collection of Voltaire's *bons mots*, but I'm afraid our readers might find them trite. Who wants Voltaire these days? What they want is a cudgel! To knock every last tooth out of each other's heads! And that's the sum total of my literary activity. Except that I also send letters to editors, gratis, over my full signature. I give reassurance and advice, and criticism and pointers. Last week I sent my fortieth letter in two years to one editor—I've spent four roubles on postage alone. I'm a bad-tempered fellow, that's the trouble.

I reckon that artist painted me not in the cause of literature but because of the two symmetrical warts on my forehead—a phenomenon, apparently. People don't have any ideas, so they go for phenomena. But how well my warts came out on the portrait—to the life! Realism, they call it.

As for madness—a lot of people have been written off as mad over the past year. And the words they use . . . 'Such an original talent . . . yet see how it turned out in the end . . . but of course the whole thing could have been predicted long ago . . .' That's pretty clever, I grant you; from a purely artistic point of view, it's quite admirable. But then they got even smarter. That's the thing; they know how to drive a man mad here, but they've never made anyone smarter.

The cleverest man of all, I reckon, is the one who calls himself a fool at least once a month. An unheard-of talent these days! In the old days, a fool might just realize he was a fool once a year, at best; but now, no chance! And they've mixed everything up so much, you can't tell a fool from a wise man any more. They've done it on purpose.

I remember a Spanish quip, when the French built their first lunatic asylum two and a half centuries ago. 'They've locked up all their fools in a special building, to prove they're wise themselves.' That's spot on: locking someone else up in an asylum doesn't prove you're wise yourself. 'K has gone mad; that means we're wise now.' No, it doesn't.

To hell with it, anyway ... why am I going on about how intelligent I am, sulking on and on. Even my maid is fed up with me. Yesterday a friend came round. 'You're changing your style,' he says. 'It's gone choppy. You chop and chop—here's an introductory sentence, but first there's another one to introduce that one, and then you shove in something else in brackets, and then you chop it some more, and chop it again ...'

My friend's right. Something strange is happening to me. My personality's changing, and my head's aching. I'm starting to see and hear strange things. Not voices, exactly, but as if there was somebody beside me: 'bobok, bobok, bobok!'

What's that all about—bobok? I need to take my mind off things.

*

I went out to take my mind off things, and ended up at a funeral. A distant relative. Still, he was a collegiate councillor. A widow, and five daughters, all unmarried. Think what it must cost, just to keep them in boots! The dead man managed it, but now—a miserable little pension. They'll have to tighten their belts.

They were never pleased to see me when I went round. And I wouldn't have gone today, but for the special circumstances. I followed the procession to the cemetery with everyone else, but they put on airs and kept me at a distance. My uniform was certainly quite shabby. It was twenty-five years, I think, since I was last in a cemetery. What a place!

First of all, the smell. About fifteen bodies had been brought in. Palls at various prices; there were even two catafalques, one for a general and one for some lady. A lot of mournful faces, a lot of pretend mourning, and a lot of open gaiety. The clergy can't complain—that's where the money comes from. But the smell, the smell! I wouldn't like to be a priest here.

I glanced cautiously at the dead people's faces. I wasn't sure of controlling myself—I'm too sensitive. Some had gentle expressions, others unpleasant ones. The smiles weren't generally nice, and some were very far from nice. I don't like them—they give me dreams.

During the service I came out of the church for some air. The weather was grey but dry. Cold, too; it was October after all. Strolled among the graves. They have different classes of graves. Third class, thirty roubles—that's decent and not too expensive. The first two classes are inside the church and under the porch; they set you back quite a bit. Half a dozen people were getting third-class funerals that day, including the general and the lady.

I looked down into the graves—horrible! Water, and what water! Totally green, and ... well, never mind. The gravedigger kept coming back every minute to bale it out with a scoop. While the service carried on, I wandered out of the gates. There was an almshouse nearby, and a restaurant a little further on. Not a bad little place, either: they had snacks and everything. Lots of mourners there, too. I noticed a great deal of merriment, real high spirits. I had a snack and a drink there.

After that I personally lent a hand, carrying the coffin from the church to the grave. How is it that dead people in their coffins get so heavy? They say it's a kind of inertia—the body no longer obeying its owner ... or some such rubbish. It goes against mechanics and common sense. I don't like it when people with no more than a general education set themselves up to solve specialist problems, but that happens here all the time. Civilians like to sound off about a soldier's business, even a field marshal's business, while trained engineers prefer to lay down the law on philosophy and economics.

I didn't go to the wake. I'm a proud man, and if I'm only welcome because it's a special occasion, then what's the point of traipsing off to their dinners, even if they're funeral dinners? The only thing I don't understand is why I stayed behind in the cemetery. I sat down on a gravestone and let my mind wander along suitable lines.

I began with a Moscow exhibition, and ended up with astonishment—thinking about astonishment as a topic. My conclusions about 'astonishment' were the following:

'Being astonished at everything, of course, is stupid; while being astonished at nothing is far more attractive, and for some reason is accepted as good form. But that's not quite right. In my opinion, being astonished at nothing is far stupider than being astonished at everything. Indeed, being astonished at nothing is almost the same thing as respecting nothing. And a stupid person is incapable of respect.'

'What I want most of all is to feel respect,' a friend of mine said to me recently. 'I long to feel respect.'

He longs to feel respect! My God, I thought, whatever would happen to you if you dared put that down in print!

At that point my mind drifted off. I don't like reading epitaphs on gravestones—they're always the same. A half-eaten sandwich was lying on the gravestone next to me; that was silly and out of place. I flicked it off onto the ground, since it wasn't bread but merely a sandwich. In any case, I believe, dropping bread-crumbs on the ground isn't a sin—it's a sin if you drop them on the floor. Must check in Suvorin's *Almanac*.

I must have sat there a long time, too long in fact; I mean, I actually lay down on a long stone slab like a marble coffin. I don't know how it was, but I suddenly began hearing things. At first I paid no attention, and disregarded it. But the conversation went on. I could hear muffled sounds, as if the speakers' mouths were covered with pillows; and yet the sounds were quite distinct, and very close by. I came to myself, sat up and began listening carefully.

'Your Excellency, that's simply not possible. You declared hearts, I took you up, and suddenly you play the seven of diamonds. We ought to have started by agreeing on diamonds.'

'You mean, playing from memory? What's the attraction of that?'

'It's no good, your Excellency, it's no good without a guarantee. There's simply got to be a dummy, and one hand face down.'

'Well, you'll never get a dummy here.'

What arrogant words, I must say! And so odd and unexpected. One of the voices so solid and ponderous, the other sort of soft and honeyed; I'd never have believed in them, if I hadn't heard them myself. I didn't seem to be at a wake; and yet how could they be playing Preference here, and how come there was this general? The voices were coming from under the gravestones, there was no doubt about that. I bent down to read the epitaph:

'Here lies the body of Major General Pervoedov... Knight of such and such orders'. Hmm. 'Died in August of this year ... aged fifty-seven years ... Rest in peace, beloved ashes, till the joyful dawn!'

Well, blow me—a real general! The other grave, from which the obsequious voice had come, didn't have a monument yet, there was just a tombstone. Obviously a new arrival. By his voice, he must be a court councillor.

'Oh-oh-oh-oh!' came a new voice, a dozen yards from the general's place and straight from a fresh grave—a lower-class male voice, a feeble, maudlin, melting voice.

'Oh-oh-oh-oh!'

'There he goes, hiccupping again!' came the haughty, fastidious voice of an irritable society lady. 'It's such a trial, being stuck next to this shopkeeper!'

'I never hiccupped, I haven't even eaten, it's just the way I am. And you, lady, with all your fine airs, you don't seem able to control yourself at all!'

'So why did you have to come and lie here?'

'They laid me here, my wife and little children did, I didn't lie down here myself. The mystery of death! And I wouldn't have chosen to lie down next to you, not for anything, not for all the gold in town; but I'm lying here as befits my fortune, as the price dictates. That's something we can always do—save up to pay for a third-class grave.'

'So you saved up; swindled your customers, did you?'

'How could I have swindled you, when I haven't seen a penny of your money since last January? There's a little bill against you in the shop now.'

'Well that's really stupid. Trying to recover your debts down here, that's too stupid, I'd say! Go upstairs, ask my niece: she's my heiress.'

'What's the point of asking anyone, or going anywhere? We've both come to the end now, and shall be equal in our sins before the judgement seat of the Lord.'

'In our sins!' the dead lady echoed him contemptuously. 'Don't you dare say another word to me!'

'Oh-oh-oh-oh!'

'All the same, your Excellency, that shopkeeper is obeying the lady.'

'Why wouldn't he?'

'Well, everybody knows, your Excellency—there's a new order down here.'

'What sort of new order?'

'Well, we're sort of dead, so to speak, your Excellency.'

'Ah, yes! But there still has to be order . . .'

So thanks very much, that's a fine comfort, I must say! If things have come to such a pass down there, what can you expect up here? What a performance, though! But I went on listening, though I was seething with indignation.

'No, I could have lived a bit! No . . . you know, I . . . I could have lived a bit!' came a new voice, somewhere in the gap between the general and the indignant lady.

'Do you hear him, your Excellency? Our fellow's at it again. Not a word out of him for three days on end, and then he starts off—"I could have lived a bit, no, I could have lived!" And you know, so greedily, hee-hee!'

'And so frivolous.'

'It gets too much for him, your Excellency; you know, he falls asleep, fast asleep—he's been here since April, after all—and then out he comes with "I could have lived!"'

'Boring, though,' remarked his Excellency.

'Yes, it's boring, your Excellency. Shall we tease Avdotya Ignatyevna some more? Hee-hee!'

'No, spare me, do. I can't stand that stroppy harridan.'

'And I can't stand you two either,' the harridan shouted back furiously. 'You're both complete bores, and you can't say anything idealistic. I know a little story about you, your Excellency—don't put on any of your airs, please—and how one morning a footman had to sweep you out with a broom from under a certain married couple's bed.'

'Repulsive woman!' growled the general through gritted teeth.

'Avdotya Ignatyevna, my dear,' the shopkeeper wailed again, 'my dear lady, would you tell me, meaning no harm—is this the ordeal by torments that I'm going through, or is something else happening? . .'

'Oh, he's at it again—I could feel it coming, I'm getting that smell from him, that smell again—that's him turning over!'

'I'm not turning over, my dear, and I'm not giving off any particular smell, because I've kept my body whole and undamaged, and it's you, my lady, who've started going off. Because the smell here is simply unbearable, even allowing for where we are. It's only manners that make me hold my tongue.'

'Oh, you horrible, rude man! He absolutely stinks, and he goes on about me.'

'Oh-oh-oh-oh! If only my forty days were up soon! Then I should hear their tearful voices above me, my wife wailing and my children quietly weeping!'

'So that's what he's crying for! They'll just stuff their faces with funeral sweets and push off. Oh, if only someone would wake up!'

'Avdotya Ignatyevna,' began the fawning official, 'wait a little longer, and the new arrivals will start talking.'

'And are there any young people among them?'

'Yes, some of them are young, Avdotya Ignatyevna. Just lads, even.'

'Oh, how wonderful that would be!'

'What, haven't they started yet?' enquired his Excellency.

'No, even the ones from two days ago haven't come round yet, your Excellency; as you know, sometimes they don't say a word for a week. It's lucky a whole new lot were brought along, yesterday and the day before, and then today. Otherwise there's nothing but last year's, for thirty yards around.'

'Yes, that's interesting.'

'Look, your Excellency, today they buried Privy Councillor Tarasevich; I could tell by their voices. I know his nephew; he was lowering the coffin just now.'

'Hmm. So where is he now?'

'Just five paces away from you, your Excellency, on your left. Almost at your feet, sir ... You ought to make his acquaintance, your Excellency.'

'Hmm. No, no ... it's not for me to make the first move.'

'No, he'll start it off himself, your Excellency. In fact he'll be flattered, believe me, your Excellency, and I—'

'Oh dear, oh dear ... oh, what's happening to me?' groaned a new and frightened voice.

'A new one, your Excellency, a new one, thank God—and how quick! Sometimes they don't say anything for a whole week.'

'Ah, a young man, I believe!' squealed Avdotya Ignatyevna.

'I ... I ... I had complications, and so sudden!' stammered the young man again. 'Schulz told me, just the day before—you've got complications, he said; and the very next morning I died. Oh dear! Oh dear!'

'Well, nothing to be done, young man,' remarked the general in a gracious voice, evidently glad of the new arrival. 'You must take comfort. Welcome to our Vale of Jehoshaphat, as you might say. We're kind folk here, you'll appreciate us when you get to know us. Major General Vasily Vasilyevich Pervoedov at your service.'

'Oh no, no! I never could have! . . I went to Schulz, and you know, I developed a complication, first it caught me in the chest, and I had a cough, and then a chill; it was my chest, and the influenza . . . and then suddenly, quite unexpectedly . . . yes, the main thing was, it was so unexpected!'

'You say it started off in your chest . . .' the councillor put in gently, as if to reassure the newcomer.

'Yes, my chest, and the phlegm, and then suddenly there wasn't any phlegm, and my chest, and I couldn't breathe . . . and you know—'

'Yes, I know, I know. But if it was your chest, you should have gone to Eck, not Schulz.'

'Do you know, I kept meaning to go and see Botkin . . . but suddenly—'

'Well, Botkin, he stings you,' remarked the general.

'Oh no, he doesn't sting at all; I've heard he's so attentive, and tells you everything that's going to happen.'

'His Excellency was alluding to his fees,' explained the clerk.

'Oh no, what do you mean, just three roubles, and he examines you so carefully, and prescribes . . . and I was set on seeing him, because I'd been told . . . So, gentlemen, what ought I to do, go to Eck or Botkin?'

'What? Go where?' The general's corpse shook with friendly laughter. The councillor seconded him in a falsetto.

'Dear boy, my dear delightful boy, how I love you!' Avdotya Ignatyevna squealed ecstatically. 'If only they'd put someone like you next to me!'

So that's what today's dead are like! No, truly, I can't accept it! But let's go on listening, without jumping to conclusions. This snotty-nosed newcomer—I remember seeing him in his coffin earlier on—had a face like a terrified chicken, the most revolting expression you ever saw. But on we go.

The next thing to happen was that pandemonium broke out, so wild that I couldn't keep track of it, because a great many people all woke up at once. There was an official, a state councillor, who instantly began telling the general about some plans for a new subcommittee at the ministry of such-and-such affairs, and how some of the staff would probably have to be transferred because of it, all of which the general found immensely interesting. I must confess that I too discovered a lot that was new to me, and that led me to marvel at the channels through which one can sometimes catch up with administrative news in this capital city of ours.

After that an engineer half woke up, but he went on for ages, mumbling complete nonsense, so our people didn't bother him but left him lying in peace for a while. And the grand lady buried under a catafalque that morning at last also showed signs of sepulchral reanimation. Lebezyatnikov (for the obsequious court councillor whom I so detested, who lay next to General Pervoedov, turned out to be called Lebezyatnikov) made a great fuss and was very surprised that everyone was waking up so quickly today. I must say I was surprised at that myself, though as a matter of fact some of the ones just waking up had been buried as long as two days before. One of them, for instance, was a very young girl of only sixteen, who kept giggling—giggling in a horrible, hungry way.

'Your Excellency, Privy Councillor Tarasevich is waking up!' Lebezyatnikov announced hurriedly, all of a sudden.

'Eh? What's that?' the privy councillor mumbled as he awoke. He sounded like a petulant, spoilt, bossy baby. I listened, full of curiosity, for over the past few days I had heard a little about this Tarasevich—things that were both tantalizing and extremely alarming.

'This is me, your Excellency, just me for the moment.'

'What do you want? What can I do for you?'

'I just wanted to ask after your Excellency's health. Not being accustomed to these conditions, everyone feels a little cramped here to start with, sir . . . General Pervoedov requests the honour of making your Excellency's acquaintance, and hopes—'

'Never heard of him.'

'Surely, your Excellency—General Pervoedov, Vasily Vasilyevich—'

'You are General Pervoedov?'

'No sir, no, your Excellency, I'm just Court Councillor Lebezyatnikov, sir, at your service, but General Pervoedov—'

'Rubbish! Kindly leave me alone.'

'Forget it.' General Pervoedov himself at last called a halt to the repulsive wheedling of his sycophantic graveyard acolyte.

'He's not woken up yet, your Excellency, you must remember that; he's not used to all this. He'll wake up and take it differently, sir—'

'Forget it,' the general repeated.

'Vasily Vasilyevich! Hey there, your Excellency!' cried an entirely new voice, loud and excited, right next to Avdotya Ignatyevna. It was a voice full of gentlemanly insolence, fashionably languid with an arrogant drawl. 'I've been observing you all for the last two hours—for I've been here three days. You remember me, Vasily Vasilyevich? I'm Klinevich, we met at the Volokonskys', though I've no idea why they let you in there.'

'What, Count Piotr Petrovich . . . is it really you . . . and so young . . . I'm so sorry!'

'Yes, I'm sorry too, but I don't care, and I mean to make the most of wherever I am. And I'm not a count but a baron, a mere baron. We're some sort of mangy little barons, descended from flunkeys, I've no idea why, and I couldn't care less. I'm just a bad lot from pseudo high society, where they call me their "darling *polisson*". My dad's some kind of little general, and my mother was once received *en haut lieu*. Last year I got together with the Jew Ziffel to forge fifty thousand roubles in notes, and then I grassed on him, and Yulka Charpentier de Lusignan ran off to Bordeaux with all the money. And now, would you believe it, I'd got properly engaged—the Schevalevsky girl, just three months short of sixteen, still at school, dowry of ninety thousand. Avdotya Ignatyevna, remember fifteen years ago, when you seduced me while I was in the Corps of Pages, just fourteen?'

'Oh, it's you, you rascal; well, what a godsend you are; otherwise here—'

'You were wrong to suspect your neighbour, the business gentleman, of causing the bad smell . . . I was just laughing quietly to myself. It was me—in fact they had to bury me in a sealed coffin.'

'Oh, what a horrible man! But still, I'm glad you're here, Klinevich—there's so little liveliness and wit down here, you wouldn't believe it.'

'Yes indeed, yes indeed; but I mean to set up something original here. Your Excellency—I don't mean you, Pervoedov—Your Excellency, the other one, Mr Tarasevich, Privy Councillor! Are you there? I'm Klinevich, who took you to Mademoiselle Furie's last Lent, do you hear me?'

'Yes, I hear you, Klinevich, and I'm very glad . . . And believe me—'

'I don't believe a thing, and I couldn't care less. I just wish I could kiss you, you dear old man, but thank God I can't. Gentlemen, do you know what this *grand-père* pulled off? He died three or four days ago, and would you believe it, he left the accounts short of a whole four hundred thousand roubles of government money! The widows' and orphans' fund, for which he had sole responsibility, for some reason, so it hadn't been audited for the last eight years. Just imagine what long faces they'll be wearing now, and the names they'll be calling him! A delicious thought, isn't it? I've spent all last year wondering how an ancient seventy-year-old riddled with gout and rheumatism could have preserved so much energy for his debaucher-ies—and here's the answer! Those widows and orphans—the mere thought of them must have got him red-hot! . . I've known about it for ages, I was the only one to know; Yulka Charpentier passed it on to me, and as soon as I found out, I paid him a visit in Easter week and leant on him, in a friendly way: "Hand over twenty-five thousand, or you'll have the auditors round tomorrow." And believe it or not, by then he had only thirteen thousand left, so it looks as if he died in the nick of time. *Grand-père, grand-père*, do you hear me?'

'*Cher* Klinevich, I absolutely agree with you, but there was no need to . . . go into all those details. Life holds so much suffering, so much torment, and offers so little reward . . . I wished to have some peace at last; and as far as I can see, I hope to get all I can out of this place too . . .'

'I bet he's already sniffed out Katiche Berestova!'

'Who? . . What Katiche?' came the old man's quavering, hungry voice.

'Aha! What Katiche? Right here, on the left, five steps from me, and ten from you. It's her fifth day down here, and if you only knew, *grand-père*, what a little rogue she is . . . from a good family, well-bred, and—a monster, a monster of the first water! I would never let anyone see her out there, I was the only one who knew her . . . Katiche, are you there?'

'Hee-hee-hee!' came the girl's reply, in a grating voice that yet had something needle-sharp to it. 'Hee-hee-hee!'

'And she's a ... little ... blonde?' quavered the *grand-père*, with a gasp between each word.

'Hee-hee-hee!'

'I've always ... always dreamt ... of a little blonde ...' the old man stammered breathlessly, 'a fifteen-year-old ... and in just this kind of situation ...'

'Oh you monster!' exclaimed Avdotya Ignatyevna.

'That'll do!' Klinevich declared. 'I can see we've got first-rate material. We'll set everything up straight away, in the best possible way. The main thing is to have all the fun we can for the rest of our time here. But how long have we got? Hey you, the official or whatever you are, Lebezyatnikov, I think I heard them call you ...'

'Yes, Lebezyatnikov, Semyon Yevseich, Court Councillor, sir, at your service, and very, very pleased to serve you.'

'I don't care a toss if you're pleased or not, but you seem to know all about this place. Tell me, to start off with (I've been wondering since yesterday), how is it we're talking down here? We've died, but we're still talking; and we seem to be moving about too, but at the same time we're not talking and not moving either. What's the secret?'

'Well, Baron, if you wanted, Platon Nikolaevich could have explained it to you better than me.'

'Who's Platon Nikolaevich? Don't mumble, get to the point.'

'Platon Nikolaevich, our home-grown philosopher here, natural scientist and university graduate. He's published a number of books on philosophy, but he's been here three months and he's falling asleep, so there's no way of waking him up now. Once a week he mumbles a few words, but there's no sense to them.'

'Get on with it!'

'He explains it all by one very simple fact: up there, when we were still alive, we mistakenly regarded our death as death. Here, the body seems to revive again, the remnants of life become concentrated, but only in our consciousness. That . . . I don't know how to put it . . . extends our life by some process of inertia. Everything gets concentrated, he says, somewhere in our consciousness, and goes on for another two or three months . . . sometimes even half a year . . . There's someone here, for instance, who's almost completely decomposed, but once every six weeks or so he suddenly comes out with one word, quite meaningless of course, about a bean, some sort of "bobok"—"Bobok, bobok," he goes—meaning that even in him, there's a minute spark of life still glimmering . . .'

'That's pretty stupid. Well, and how come I've got no sense of smell, but I can still detect a stink?'

'Well, that . . . heh-heh . . . well, as to that, our philosopher got a bit foggy. He commented that the stink you smell here is what you might call a moral stench—heh-heh! It's the stench of the soul, he says, meaning that the soul has these two or three months to reform itself . . . and that's the final mercy, so to speak . . . Only it seems to me, Baron, that all this is no more than mystical ravings, of course quite excusable in his situation.'

'That's enough; I'm sure the rest is all nonsense. The main thing is, we've got two or three months of life, and at the end of it all—bobok. I suggest we all spend these two months as pleasantly as we can, and with that in mind we should set everything up on a different basis. Ladies and gentlemen! I propose that we cast aside all shame!'

'Oh yes, do let's cast aside all shame! Do let's!' echoed a multitude of voices; and strange to say, there were some entirely new ones to be heard—evidently people who had meanwhile just woken up. The engineer, who was by now completely awake, roared his approval with particular eagerness, in a thundering bass voice. The girl Katiche giggled with delight.

'Ah, how I long to cast aside all shame!' cried Avdotya Ignatyevna ecstatically.

'D'you hear that? Well, if even Avdotya Ignatyevna wants to cast aside all shame . . .'

'No-no-no, Klinevich, I did have shame, I really did have some shame up there, but here I terribly, terribly want not to be ashamed of anything!'

'I understand, Klinevich,' boomed the engineer, 'that you propose to organize our local life, as it were, along new and rational lines.'

'I don't give a toss for that! As far as that goes, let's wait for Kudeyarov, they brought him in yesterday. He'll wake up and explain everything. He's such a personality, such a gigantic personality! And tomorrow, I believe, they're going to drag along another scientist, and an officer for certain, and if I'm not mistaken, in another three or four days there'll be a gossip columnist, and I think his editor too. Anyway, to hell with them, but we'll all get together in a group, and sort everything out among ourselves. But meanwhile I want no lying. That's all I want, because it's the most important thing. Living on the earth without lying is impossible—living and lying are synonymous; but down here we can amuse ourselves by not lying.

Damn it all, the grave does mean something, doesn't it! We'll all tell our stories out loud, without being ashamed of anything. I'll start by telling you about myself. You know, I was one of the predators. Everything up there was tied up in rotten ropes. Away with the ropes!—And let's spend these two months in the most shameless truthfulness! Let's strip off and get naked!'

'Yes, get naked! Get naked!' cried all the voices.

'I'm so longing, so longing to get naked!' squealed Avdotya Ignatyevna.

'Oh . . . Oh . . . Oh, I can see it's all going to be such fun here! I don't want to go and see Eck!'

'No, I could have lived, no, you know, I could have lived!'

'Hee-hee-hee' giggled Katiche.

'The main thing is that no one can stop us; and though I can see Pervoedov is annoyed, I'm out of his reach. *Grand-père*, are you with us?'

'I'm totally, totally with you, with the very greatest pleasure, only on condition that Katiche starts off by giving us her own bi-o-graphy.'

'I protest! I protest most strongly!' announced General Pervoedov firmly.

'Your Excellency!' the villain Lebezyatnikov pleaded anxiously, dropping his voice to a hurried, yammering undertone. 'Your Excellency, it'll really be better for us if we agree. You know there's that girl here ... and after all, there were all those little affairs ...'

'Well yes, the girl, but—'

'It'll be better for us, your Excellency, by God it'll be better! Let's give it a try at least, just give it a go ...'

'Even in the grave, they won't let me rest!'

'Firstly, General, there you were, playing Preference in your grave; and secondly, we don't give a damn about you!' drawled Klinevich.

'My dear sir, pray do not forget yourself.'

'What? But I'm out of your reach, and I can tease you from here like Yulka's lapdog. Besides, gentlemen, what kind of a general is he down here? Up there he was a general, but here he's rubbish.'

'No, I'm not rubbish ... even here—'

'Here you'll rot in your coffin, and there'll be nothing left but half a dozen brass buttons.'

'Bravo, Klinevich, ha-ha-ha!' roared the voices.

'I served my sovereign ... I carry a sword ...'

'Your sword will do for skewering mice, and anyway, you never drew it in your life.'

'That makes no difference, sir; I was a part of the whole.'

'There are all sorts of parts of a whole.'

'Bravo, Klinevich, bravo, ha-ha-ha!'

'I don't understand what a sword is for,' declared the engineer.

'We'll run away from the Prussians like mice, they'll crush us to dust!' cried a distant voice I didn't recognize, literally spluttering with delight.

'A sword, my good sir, denotes honour,' the general cried, but I was the only one to hear him. A long-drawn-out, wild bellowing, a hubbub and uproar broke out, in which all I could make out were the hysterical, impatient screams of Avdotya Ignatyevna.

'Come along! Hurry up! Oh, when are we going to start casting aside all shame!'

'Oh-oh-oh! Verily my soul is passing through the torments!' came the voice of the plain man. And then . . .

And then suddenly I sneezed. It was involuntary and unexpected, but the effect was astounding. All the noise instantly ceased, as if in a graveyard; everything vanished like a dream. A real silence of the tomb descended. I don't think they were ashamed in my presence—after all, they had resolved not to be ashamed of anything! I waited another five minutes, but—not a word, not a sound. And one couldn't suppose they were frightened of being reported to the police—for what could the police have done? I'm forced to conclude that they must possess some secret unknown to the living, which they carefully conceal from every mortal being.

'Well, my dears,' I thought to myself, 'I'll come and visit you again.' And with that I left the cemetery.

No, this I can't allow! I really can't! I'm not bothered by bobok. (So that's what bobok was all about!)

Debauchery in a place like that—debauchery of their last hopes, debauchery by a lot of flaccid putrefying corpses—not even sparing their last conscious moments! They're given, they're granted those last moments, and ... And worst of all, worse than anything—in such a place! No, that I can't accept.

I'll visit other classes of graves. I'll listen everywhere. That's the thing—you have to listen everywhere, not just in one spot, to get a proper idea. Who knows, I may happen upon something reassuring.

But I'll definitely go back to that lot. They promised their biographies, and all kinds of anecdotes. Ugh! But I'll go back, I definitely will, it's a matter of conscience!

I'll take it to *The Citizen*. One of the editors had his portrait exhibited there too. Perhaps he'll print it.

A MEEK CREATURE

A Fantasy

FROM THE AUTHOR

ABOUT THE STORY: I have given it the title of *A Fantasy*, although I consider it entirely realistic. But there is some fantasy in it, in the very form of the work, and this needs to be explained before I start.

The point is that this is not exactly a story, nor a set of notes. Picture to yourselves a man confronted by his wife lying on his table, having killed herself a few hours before by throwing herself out of a window. He is in a bewildered state, not yet able to collect his thoughts. He wanders from one room to another, trying to make sense of what has happened, to 'pull his thoughts together into one point'. Now he is an inveterate fantasist, one of those men who talk to themselves aloud. And here he is, talking to himself, telling the whole story and trying to explain it to himself. Although what he says hangs together, he contradicts himself several times, both as to logic and emotions. He defends himself, and accuses her, and gets sidetracked; we see the coarseness of his mind and heart, alongside deep feeling. Little by little, he does explain the event to himself, and gathers his thoughts 'into one point'. He calls up a series of memories which bring him irresistibly to the truth at last; and the truth irresistibly elevates his mind and heart. By the end, the very tone of the story has changed from its chaotic beginning. The truth opens itself up to this unfortunate man—quite clearly and manifestly, for him at least.

That's the topic. Of course the account itself takes several hours, in disorganized scraps and fragments: sometimes he's talking to himself, sometimes he seems to be addressing an invisible listener, a sort of judge. But reality is always like that. If a stenographer had been listening to him and writing everything down, it would have come out rougher and less polished than in my account; but I believe that the psychological structure might well have turned out the same. And it is this idea of a stenographer recording everything (after which I would have organized what he had taken down) that constitutes what I call the fantasy element in this story. This sort of approach has been repeatedly used in literature; Victor Hugo, for instance, in his masterpiece *The Last Day of a Condemned Man*, uses almost the same technique, imagining that a condemned man could (and would have time to) note everything down not only on his last day, but in his last hour and even his very last minute. Yet if he had not allowed himself this fantasy, the whole work could never have existed—the most realistic and truthful work that he ever wrote.

CHAPTER ONE

I. Who I Was and Who She Was

. . . While she's here, everything is still all right; I keep coming back to look at her every minute; but tomorrow they'll take her away, and—how can I carry on alone? Right now she's on a table in the big room, they've put two card tables together; but the coffin will arrive tomorrow, it's lined with white Naples silk—well, what does it matter . . . I keep walking round, I want to sort it all out for myself. Six hours I've been trying, but I still can't pull my thoughts together into one point. The thing is, I keep pacing round, and pacing, and pacing . . . This is how it all was. I'll go through everything in order (order, indeed!). Gentlemen, I'm not a literary man, you can see that for yourselves, but never mind; I'll tell you everything the way I understand it myself. Because that's the whole horror of it—I understand it all!

If you want to know, I mean if I'm to start at the very beginning, she just simply came in to pawn a few things, to pay for a notice in *The Voice* saying this and that, offering her services as a governess, will travel, qualified to give home tuition, et cetera, et cetera. That was right at the start, and obviously she seemed no different from the others—she came along just like everybody else, well, and so on. And then I did start to see a difference. She was a thinnish sort of girl, fair-haired, tallish. With me, she was always a bit awkward, as if she was embarrassed (I think she was the same with everyone else too; and obviously from her point of view I was no different from anyone else, I mean as a human being, not a pawnbroker). As soon as she got her money, she turned and left at once. Never said a word. Other people—they argue, ask for more, try to haggle with you, but not this one—she took whatever she was given . . . I'm getting muddled, I think . . . Oh yes, it was her offerings that struck me to start with—silver gilt earrings, a wretched little medallion, tuppenny stuff. And she knew that was all it was worth, but I could see on her face that the things were precious to her—and true enough, they were all she had left from her papa and mama, I found that out later. Just once, I allowed myself a condescending smile at her things. I mean to say, see, I never let myself do that. I have a gentlemanly way with my customers: few words, polite, but stern. 'Stern, stern, stern!' But this time she had allowed herself to bring along the remains (yes, literally the remains) of an old rabbit-skin jacket—and I couldn't help myself, I suddenly came out with something, a sort of joke. Oh my, how she flared up! She had big, blue, pensive eyes—but how they blazed! Didn't say a word, picked up the 'remains', and walked out. That was the first time I really noticed her, and thought about her in that way, I mean that particular way. And I remember my impression of her—I mean my main impression, if you like, the one that summed it all up: she was terribly young, so young, she seemed to be only fourteen. Though actually at the time she was just three months short of sixteen. But no, that wasn't what I wanted to say at all, that wasn't what summed it up. The next day she came back. Later I discovered that she'd been to Dobronravov, and to Moser as well, and taken them that jacket; only they don't take anything but gold, and wouldn't even speak to her. Whereas I had once accepted a cameo from her (a wretched one), and later when I realized what I'd done, I was surprised at myself. I don't accept anything but gold or silver either, and yet I'd taken her cameo. That was my second thought about her then, I remember that.

This time, I mean after Moser, she brought an amber cigar holder—not a bad little thing, someone could have fancied it, but it wasn't worth anything to me, I only take gold. And since this visit of hers came on top of yesterday's revolt, I received her sternly. What I mean by sternly is that I was cold with her. But when I handed her the two roubles, I couldn't resist saying with some annoyance, 'I'm only doing this *for you*; Moser would never take such a thing from you.' I emphasized the words 'for you', and I said them in that certain way. I was angry. She flared up again when I said 'for you', but held her tongue, didn't throw down the money, took it . . . that's poverty for you! But how she flared up! I could see I'd needled her. And then after she'd gone, I suddenly asked myself: was that triumph over her really worth two roubles? He-he-he! I remember asking myself that same question twice over: 'Was it worth it? Was it worth it?' And I laughed, and answered myself in the affirmative. I was very tickled indeed. But it wasn't a bad feeling.

What I did had been on purpose, by design: I had wanted to test her, because some ideas about her were beginning to brew in my mind. That was my third particular thought about her.

Well, it all started from there. Naturally I tried at once to find out about her circumstances from other people; and I waited very eagerly for her next visit. I had a feeling she'd come back soon. When she came, I struck up a friendly conversation with her, being unusually polite. I mean, I wasn't badly brought up, I have good manners. Hmm. And now I realized that she was kind and meek. Kind and meek people can't hold out for long; although they never open up very much, they can't quite manage to get out of a conversation. They give grudging answers, but they do answer, and the longer the conversation goes on, the more they say; only you mustn't tire of the conversation if there's something you need to know. At the time, naturally, she herself never explained anything. I found out about *The Voice* and the rest later on. She was making a last push to advertise—to start with, her notices had been supercilious: 'Governess,' they said, 'willing to relocate, send letter with conditions of employment'; but later on they said 'Willing to take on any work, teaching, or as companion, keeping house, caring for an invalid, some sewing . . .' et cetera, et cetera, all the same old things! Of course all these things got added to the advertisements bit by bit, and by the end, when she was really desperate, they said 'no wages, just my keep'. No, she never got offered a place! I decided to test her one last time. I brought her that day's *The Voice* and showed her an advertisement: 'Young person, orphan, seeks place as governess to small children, preferably with an older widower. Can assist with housework.'

'See that? It was published this morning, and she'll have found a situation by evening. That's the way to advertise!'

She flared up again, eyes blazing once more, turned and walked out. I really liked that. Actually I was quite certain of everything by then, I had no fears. No one was going to take her cigar holders. She had run out of cigar holders by then anyway. And sure enough, she turned up again two days later, so pale and agitated—I realized that something had happened at her home, and so it had. I'll explain what it was shortly, but just now I want to describe how I showed myself to be high-minded, and raised my standing in her eyes. I suddenly decided to do it. The thing was that she brought in this icon (she had plucked up her courage to bring it) . . . Oh, listen, listen! Now it's all started coming back, I've been quite muddled up till now . . .

The thing is that now I want to remember all of it, every detail of it, every pen stroke. I want to bring my thoughts to a point, but—I can't; it's all these little pen strokes, little pen strokes . . .

It was an icon of the Mother of God. The Mother of God with the Child, a homely, old-fashioned one, in a silver gilt setting; worth—well—say six roubles. I could see it was precious to her; she was pawning the whole icon, without taking it out of its setting. I told her she'd better remove the icon from its setting, and take it back home; it was an icon, after all.

'Why,' she says, 'aren't you allowed to take them?'

'No, it's not that, but perhaps you yourself might . . .'

'Well, take it out, then.'

'You know what?' I said on reflection, 'I shan't take it out of its setting. I'll put it over there on the stand, with the other icons, under the lamp' (I'd always had an icon lamp burning there, ever since I opened my shop), 'and you can just take ten roubles.'

'I don't want ten, give me five. I'll definitely redeem it.'

'Don't you want ten? The icon is worth it,' I added, seeing her eyes flash again. She said nothing. I brought her out five roubles.

'Never despise anyone; I've been in the same fix myself, and worse. If you see me in this business now . . . well, that's after all the other things I've been through . . .'

'Getting your revenge on society? Is that it?' she suddenly interrupted me, with rather acid mockery, though with a good deal of innocence to it too; it was a general comment, because she didn't make the least distinction between me and anyone else, so it came out without any real malice. 'Aha!' I thought, 'so that's what you're like. Your character's coming out now—a new woman.'

'You see,' I answered at once, half joking and half mysterious. '*I am a part of that part of the whole which seeks to do evil, yet always does good.*'

She looked quickly at me, with a marked curiosity that was somehow very childlike.

'Wait a minute . . . What's that idea? Where's it from? I've heard it somewhere before . . .'

'No need to rack your brains, those are the words Mephistopheles uses to commend himself to Faust. Have you read *Faust*?'

'No . . . not attentively.'

'You mean you haven't read it at all. You should. But I can see that mocking curl of your lips again. Please don't imagine I'm so tasteless as to present myself to you as a Mephistopheles, just to glamorize my role as a pawnbroker. A pawnbroker I am, and a pawnbroker I'll always be. I know that.'

'You're odd, somehow . . . I never meant to say anything like that . . .'

She meant to say—I never expected you to be an educated person; she didn't say it, but I knew that was what she thought. She was dreadfully pleased with me.

'You see,' I remarked, 'one can do good in any calling. I'm not talking about myself, of course; I suppose I never do anything but harm, but—'

'Of course one can do good wherever one is,' she said, casting me a quick, penetrating look. 'Yes, wherever one is,' she suddenly repeated. O, I remember that, I remember all those moments. And I want to add that when these young things, these sweet young things, want to say something very intelligent and perceptive, their faces suddenly tell you, all too candidly and naïvely, 'here you are, I'm telling you something intelligent and perceptive!'—and that's not out of vanity, as it would be with my sort of person— but because (as you can clearly see) they themselves value all that so highly, and believe in it, and respect it, and they think that you, too, must respect it just as they do. Oh, the sincerity! That's how they win us over. And how lovely it was in her!

I remember it all, I haven't forgotten a thing! As soon as she left, I made up my mind. And that same day I went to make my final enquiries, to get all the intimate details about her and her present life. I had already found out all about her past life from Lukerya, who used to be their servant; I had bribed her a few days before. These intimate details were so terrible, I just can't understand how she could laugh, as she had just been laughing, and asking curious questions about Mephistopheles's speech, when she herself was suffering such horrors. But—youth! That was exactly what I thought about her, with pride and happiness—because that shows greatness of spirit, doesn't it? Here you are, on the brink of destruction, and yet Goethe's great words still shine out to you. Youth always possesses greatness of spirit, however faint or distorted. I mean, I'm talking about her, nobody else. And the main thing was, by then I already thought of her as mine, I had no doubt of my power. You know, it's a most voluptuous thought, once you no longer have any doubts.

But what's the matter with me? If I go on like this, when shall I ever gather my thoughts to a point? Hurry up, hurry—this isn't it, not at all! O God!

II. A Marriage Proposal

I'll sum up in a single word those 'intimate details' I found out about her: her father and mother had both died a long time ago, three years ago in fact, and she had been left in the care of two disreputable aunts. I mean, calling them disreputable is putting it too mildly. One of them was a widow with a big family, six children, each one younger than the next; the other was a spinster, a horrible old maid. Both of them were horrible. Her father had been in the civil service, a clerk, a gentleman with no hereditary title. In other words, everything played into my hands. I came into her life like someone from a higher sphere—I was, after all, a retired staff captain from a brilliant regiment, a hereditary nobleman, independent and so forth; and as for my pawnbroking business, the aunts could only look on that with respect. She had been her aunts' slave for three years, but even so she'd managed to pass an exam somewhere—she'd succeeded in doing it, driven herself to do it, while weighed down with her merciless daily grind—surely that must have said something about how hard she was striving for a better and nobler life! After all, why did I want to get married? No, forget about me—we'll come back to that . . . And was that the point anyway? She had to teach the aunt's children, do the sewing, and by the end it wasn't just the sewing—with her bad chest, she had to scrub the floors too. And they actually beat her, and openly begrudged her every mouthful she ate. In the end, they started planning to sell her. Ugh! I'll skip the ugly details. She told me all about it afterwards. A neighbour of theirs, a fat shopkeeper—not a small-time shopkeeper, he had two grocer's shops—had been watching all this going on for a whole year. He'd already charmed two wives to death, and now he was looking for a third, and she had caught his eye. 'She's quiet,' he thought, 'raised in poverty; I'll be marrying her for the orphans' sake.' That was true, he did have orphan children. So he proposed, and set about making arrangements with the aunts. He was fifty, by the way. She was in despair. That was when she started coming to me, to pay for advertisements in *The Voice*. At last she begged the aunts to give her just a bit of time to think it over. They let her have that—just one bit of time. They wouldn't let her have a second bit; they began nagging her: 'We don't know where to find food for ourselves, let alone with an extra mouth to feed!' I already knew all this, and that day, after what had happened in the morning, I made up my mind. The shopkeeper came round to their house that evening, bringing fifty kopeks' worth of sweets from his shop, and she was sitting with him, and I called Lukerya out of the kitchen and told her to go and whisper to her that I was waiting by the gate and had something urgent to say to her. I was very pleased with myself. In fact I was awfully pleased with myself all that day.

She was astonished when I called her outside. Right there, by the gate, and in Lukerya's presence, I explained that I would count it an honour and a happiness ... And secondly, I told her not to be surprised at my manner, or at my talking to her by the gate: I was a straightforward man, I said, and had found out her present situation. And I wasn't lying when I called myself straightforward. Well, what does it matter? And I did more than speak formally to her, I mean, in a way that showed I was well bred: I spoke elegantly, and that was the main thing. Why, is it a sin to admit that? I want to judge myself, and so I do. I have to speak *pro* and *contra*, and I do. Even later on, I enjoyed thinking back to that occasion, though that was silly of me: I told her straight out, quite without embarrassment, firstly that I wasn't particularly talented, nor particularly clever, nor, perhaps, particularly kind; that I was a pretty cheap egoist (I remember that phrase—I thought it up on the way, and was pleased with it); and that it might be, it might very well be, that I had many other unpleasant sides to my character too. All that was said with a special sort of pride—we all know how one says that sort of thing. And of course I had enough good taste not to go on about my virtues, once I had honourably set out my defects: not to say, 'But on the other hand, I do have this, that and the other.' I could see that she was still terribly afraid, but I didn't mince my words; in fact, seeing her fear, I purposely exaggerated things. I told her straight out, she'd have enough to eat, but as for dresses, theatres, balls—there would be none of that, at least until later on, when I had achieved what I wanted. I got really carried away with talking so severely. And I added, as casually as I could, that if I had taken up my line of business, I mean keeping a pawnbroker's shop, it was because I had a special purpose—there was a particular circumstance, I hinted . . . But I was quite within my rights to say those things: I really did have such a purpose, and there was such a circumstance. Just a minute, gentlemen—I've always hated this pawnbroker's business worse than anyone, but the fact is, though it's ridiculous to talk to myself in this mysterious way, I really was 'getting my revenge on society', I truly was, truly, truly! So her jibe that morning about my getting my revenge had been unfair. Or rather, you see, if I'd told her straight out,

'Yes, I'm getting my revenge on society,' she'd have laughed just as she did that morning, and it really would have been funny. Still, by dropping oblique hints and mysterious phrases, it turned out that I could work on her imagination. Besides which, by then I had nothing to fear; I knew that she found the fat shopkeeper even more repulsive than me, and when I came and stood by her garden gate, I appeared as her deliverer. Of course I saw that. Oh yes, a man is particularly good at seeing his own underhand behaviour! But was it underhand? How is a man to be judged here? Wasn't I in love with her already?

Wait a minute. Of course I never breathed a word to her about being her benefactor—oh no, on the contrary: 'It's you who are my benefactress, not the other way round.' I actually said that in so many words, I couldn't stop myself; and maybe it sounded rather stupid, because I noticed her face twitch a little. But all in all, I had definitely won the day. Just a minute—if I'm to go over all that muck, let me remember the final straw. As I stood there, I had these thoughts passing through my mind: you're tall, well built, cultured—without trying to boast, you're a good-looking fellow. That's what I was thinking. Needless to say, she said 'yes' to me right there, by the gate. But ... but I must add this: while she was standing by the gate, she thought long and hard before saying 'yes'. She pondered, and pondered, for such a long time that I was on the point of asking her 'Well, then?'—in fact I couldn't stop myself, I did ask her 'Well, what's it to be, miss?'—with a bit of a flourish.

'Wait a minute, I'm thinking.'

And her little face was so serious, so serious—I might have read it even then! But I was hurt: 'Can she really be choosing between me and the shopkeeper?' Oh, I didn't understand her then! I didn't understand anything yet, anything at all! Right up till today, I didn't understand! I remember Lukerya running out after me, when I was already leaving; she stopped me on the road and panted out: 'God will reward you, sir, for taking our dear young lady—only don't tell her that, she's proud.'

Proud, is she? I like proud people myself. Proud ones are particularly fine when . . . well, when you no longer doubt your own power over them, eh? Oh, you despicable blunderer! Oh, how pleased I was with myself! Do you know—when she was standing and hesitating by the gate that time, wondering whether to say yes to me, and I was puzzled by her, do you know, she might even have been thinking something like this: 'If I'm going to be miserable whichever one I choose, wouldn't it be best to choose the worse one—the fat shopkeeper—and let him beat me to death in a drunken rage and have done with it!' Eh? What do you say—could she have been thinking something like that?

Even now, I don't understand. Even now, I don't understand a thing! As I've only just said, she might have had that idea—choosing the worse of two calamities, meaning the shopkeeper. But who was worse for her just then—me or the shopkeeper? The shopkeeper, or the pawnbroker who quoted Goethe? Now that's a question! What a question! And even that you don't understand: the answer is lying on that table, and you're calling it a 'question'! But to hell with me! It's not about me at all . . . Although what have I got left now—is that something to do with me, or isn't it? Now that's what I can't decide at all. Better go to bed. My head aches . . .

III. *The Noblest of Men; though I Don't Believe It Myself*

I didn't sleep. How could I have, with that throbbing in my head? I want to make sense of it, all that filth. Oh, the filth! Oh, the filth I dragged her out of that day! Surely she must have understood that, she must have appreciated what I had done! There were other thoughts that appealed to me too, for instance that I was forty-one and she was only just sixteen. That fascinated me, that feeling of inequality—it was just delicious, quite delicious.

Another thing, I wanted a wedding *à l'anglaise*, I mean just the two of us, with only two witnesses, with Lukerya as one of them, and then straight onto the train, perhaps no further than Moscow (for I happened to have business there too), and a hotel, for a fortnight or so. But she wouldn't have it, she wouldn't let me do it, and I had to pay the aunts a respectful visit as if they were family I was taking her from. I let her have her way, and gave those aunts their due. I even made those creatures a present of a hundred roubles each, and promised them more, without telling her anything about it so as not to rub her nose in the poverty of her home. So the aunts were as soft as silk from the start. And there was an argument about her dowry too: she had nothing, almost literally nothing, but she didn't want anything either. Even so, I managed to prove to her that it wouldn't do to have nothing at all, so I gave her a dowry myself, because who else would have done anything for her? Well, but never mind about me. I did tell her some of my ideas, just to put her in the picture. Perhaps I was too hasty about that. The main thing was—right from the start, though she tried to hold back, she would hurry to greet me, full of love; she met me joyfully when I came home in the evenings, and chattered to me about herself (that enchanting innocent chatter of hers!), about her childhood, her babyhood, her parents' home, her father and mother. But I poured cold water on all that excitement of hers straight away. That was my whole idea. I greeted her raptures with silence—benevolent silence, of course . . . all the same, she soon realized that we two were different, and that I was an enigma for her. Actually, I had staked everything on being an enigma! Perhaps I had only ever gone in for this stupid scheme to make myself into an enigma! Sternness above all— so I brought her into my home in an atmosphere of sternness. In fact, although I was quite content at the time, I set up a whole system in my home. Oh, it all came about with no effort at all. It couldn't have been otherwise—I had to create that system, because of one thing that couldn't be avoided—why on earth should I be slandering myself! The system was a genuine one. No, listen—if you're going to judge a man, then judge him in full knowledge of the facts . . . Listen to me.

Where shall I start? It's very difficult. When you try to justify yourself, that's when it gets difficult. You see—young people despise money, for instance—and I emphasized the money side straight away, I laid the stress on money. And I stressed it so hard that she became more and more silent. Opened her eyes wide, listened, looked and said nothing. You see, young people are big-hearted—the good ones, that is—big-hearted and impulsive, but they're not very tolerant when things aren't to their liking; and they're scornful. And I wanted her to be broad-minded, I wanted to plant that broad-mindedness, deep in her heart, to graft it into her innermost feelings, don't you see? Just to take an ordinary example—how should I explain my pawnbroker's business to a character like hers? Naturally I didn't start straight off, talking about it, or it would have looked as if I was making excuses for the pawnshop; no, I spoke of it with pride, as it were, and I talked of it almost without words. I'm an expert at talking in silence, I've talked through my whole life in silence, I've lived in silence through whole tragedies in my life. Oh, I've been unhappy too, haven't I? I've been cast out by everybody, cast out and forgotten, and nobody, nobody at all knows that! And later this sixteen-year-old girl suddenly got hold of details of my life from bad people, and thought she knew all about me, but the most precious part of it stayed hidden here, in this heart! I kept silent, particularly with her, most particularly with her, right up to yesterday—why was I silent? Because I was proud. I wanted her to find out for herself, without my help—but not through bad people's gossip—for her to find out for herself about this man, and understand him! When I received her into my home, I wanted her to respect me completely. I wanted her to stand before me in adoration for all my suffering—and I deserved it! Oh, I've always been proud, I've always wanted to have all or nothing! Where happiness was concerned, I wouldn't accept half measures, I wanted it all; and that was the whole reason why I had to act as I did then. 'Work it out for yourself,' I thought, 'and appreciate me!' Because you must see that if I'd started explaining things to her myself, and telling her what to feel, and lowering myself and begging for respect—it would have been no different from begging for charity. Though ... Though—why talk about that, what's the point?

How stupid, stupid, stupid and stupid! I explained to her then, plainly and mercilessly (and I stress the word 'mercilessly'), in a couple of words, that young people's big-heartedness was all very fine, but not worth a brass farthing. Why not? Because they've got it on the cheap, they've never lived to earn it; for them it's no more than 'life's first impressions', as it were. Now let's see them at work! Cheap big-heartedness is always easy, even giving your life is easy, because it just means your blood's hot and you're brimming with energy, and longing passionately for beauty! No, you take a big-hearted deed that's difficult, and quiet, not known, not glamorous, slandered, demanding a lot of sacrifice and not an atom of glory—one where you, a splendid person, are despised by everyone as a villain, although you're the most honourable man in the world—just you try a deed like that! No, you'll give up! But as for me—I've done nothing else all my life but carry a deed like that on my shoulders. At first she argued with me—and how she argued!—but then she would turn quiet, completely silent, just opening her eyes dreadfully wide, and listening, with those wide, wide eyes, all attention. And . . . and on top of that, I suddenly saw a smile, a suspicious, silent, nasty smile. And it was with that smile on her face that I brought her into my home. True, she had nowhere else to go.

IV. Plans and More Plans

Which of us was the first to start it?

Neither of us. It started on its own, right from the beginning. I've said that I brought her into my home in a spirit of sternness, but I softened that straight away. Even before we were married, I had explained that she'd be accepting pledges and paying out money, and at the time she said nothing (note that). What's more, she took up the work quite enthusiastically. The apartment, the furnishings, all that, stayed as it was, of course. The apartment consists of two rooms: one is a big room, with the shop counter partitioned off, and the other—also a big room—is our living room and bedroom. I don't have much furniture: even the aunts had better stuff. My icon stand with its little lamp is in the first room, where the shop is; my own room has my bookcase, with a number of books in it, and a trunk (I keep the keys), and, well, the bed, and the tables and chairs. I told her before we were married that there would be one rouble a day, and no more, for our housekeeping—meaning food for me, her and Lukerya, whom I had poached to work for us. 'I need to have saved thirty thousand in three years,' I said, 'and we'll never save that money if we spend more.' She didn't object, but I myself raised the daily allowance by thirty kopeks. Same for the theatre. I told my fiancée there would be no theatre outings, but then I laid down that there would be one outing a month, with proper seats in the stalls. We went to three performances together, to see *The Hunt for Happiness* and *Singing Birds*, I believe (oh, confound it, what does it matter?). We went there in silence, and came back in silence. Why, oh why did we have those silences, right from the start? In those days, I remember, she was always watching me, somehow stealthily, and as soon as I noticed that, I became even more silent. There were no quarrels at first—just silence. Actually it was I who imposed the silence. She herself had suddenly rushed to embrace me a couple of times, on impulse; but as those impulses had been morbid, hysterical ones, when what I needed from her was secure happiness and respect—I received them coldly. And I turned out to be right—every one of those impulsive gestures was followed by a quarrel next day.

Or rather—there weren't any actual quarrels, but there was silence; and she began to look more and more defiant. 'Rebellion and independence', that's what it was; only she didn't know how to do it. Yes, that meek little face was growing more and more defiant. Would you believe it—she was becoming disgusted with me; I worked that out. And she began getting furious and losing her temper, there was no doubt about that. Once she had escaped from her filthy and destitute situation, even having to scrub the floors—how could she suddenly start turning her nose up at our poverty! Look, it wasn't poverty at all, it was economy; and when necessary, we even had luxuries: for instance the linen, or the cleanliness of our home. I had always dreamt, even before this, that cleanliness in a husband attracts a wife. Actually she wasn't complaining about our poverty, but what she called the stinginess of my economies. 'He has his goals,' she should have been thinking, 'he's demonstrating his firm character.' All of a sudden she refused to go to the theatre any more. And more and more often, that twisted mocking smile of hers. So I made myself still more silent. Still more silent.

I don't have to justify myself, do I? The main thing here was the pawnshop. Allow me—I knew that a woman, let alone a sixteen-year-old girl, has got to be totally subordinate to a man. There's no originality in a woman, that's axiomatic—even now, even now, I see that as axiomatic! Never mind what's lying there in the next room ... truth is truth, even J.S. Mill can't go against that! And a loving woman ... O, a loving woman—she'll worship even the vices, even the wickedness of the man she loves. He himself won't ever dream up such justifications for his wickedness as she'll find for him. Yes, that's generous of her, but there's nothing original about it. It's nothing but lack of originality that's been the ruin of women. And I ask you once more—what's the use of your pointing at that table out there? Is that original, what's on the table! O—o—oh!

Listen: at the time, I was sure of her love. Why, she used to throw her arms round my neck then. So she loved me—or rather, she wanted to love me. Yes, that's how it was: she wanted to love me, she was trying to love me. And the main thing was that there wasn't any wickedness that needed her to justify it. You may say: a pawnbroker; that's what everyone says. But so what if I'm a pawnbroker? That just means that there must have been reasons to turn the most generous-hearted of men into a pawnbroker. You see, gentlemen, there are ideas . . . well, I mean, there are some particular ideas, if you pronounce them, if you express them in words, they come out terribly silly. Embarrassing. And why? No reason. Because we're all rubbish and can't bear the truth, or . . . I don't know why. I just said 'the most generous-hearted of men'; that sounds ridiculous, but actually that's just how it was. It was the truth, I mean, the most truthful, the very most truthful truth! Yes, at that time I was within my rights to open this pawnshop to provide for myself. 'You've rejected me, you have driven me out with your sneering silence. You answered my passionate pleas for friendship with insults that will stay with me for life. And so now I've a perfect right to protect myself against you, to build a wall between us, to raise those thirty thousand roubles and live out my life somewhere in the Crimea, on a southern shore, among the mountains and vineyards, on my own estate, bought with those thirty thousand roubles, and above all—far away from you, but with no hard feelings towards you; with an ideal in my soul, with the woman I love by my side, close to my heart, and a family if God grants me one—and helping the people around me.' Of course it's just as well that I'm saying all this to myself now: what could have been stupider than saying it aloud to her at the time? That's why there was that proud silence, that's why we sat in silence. For what could she have understood? Sixteen years old, in her first youth—what could she have understood of my justifications, or my suffering? Direct and straightforward, she knew nothing of life, she was full of callow, juvenile beliefs, blind as a bat like all those 'noble hearts'—and on top of it all, this pawnshop and—*basta*! (But was I a villain in my pawnshop? Couldn't she have seen how I behaved, and whether I was being too greedy?)

Oh, how awful is truth on this earth! That beauty, that meek, heavenly creature—she was a tyrant, the unbearable tyrant of my soul, my tormentor! No, I'll let myself down if I don't say it! You think I didn't love her? Who can say I didn't love her? You see, there's an irony here, the bitter irony of fate and nature! We are cursed, all human life is cursed. (And mine most of all!) I can see now that I made a mistake. Something went wrong. Everything was clear, my plan was clear as daylight: 'Stern, proud, needing no one's moral support, suffering in silence.' That was how it was—I was not lying, no, I was not lying! 'She herself will realize later on that this came from a generous heart'— but she never could realize that. 'And when one day she comes to see it, she'll treasure me ten times more, and fall to her knees in the dust, hands clasped in adoration.' That was the plan. But then I forgot something, or overlooked it. There was something I failed to do. But that's enough of that, enough. And whose pardon am I to ask now? What's done is done. Take heart, O man, and be proud! It's not your fault! . .

Yes, let me tell the truth. I'm not afraid to confront the truth, face to face. It was her fault, it was her fault!

V. *The Meek Creature Rebels*

The quarrels began when she suddenly decided to pay out loans in her own way, pricing things at more than they were worth, and a couple of times even got into an argument with me. I didn't give in. But then this captain's widow turned up.

This old woman arrived with a locket—a present from her late husband, you know, the usual thing, a keepsake. I paid out thirty roubles. She starts moaning pathetically, begging me to hold on to it—of course, I say, we won't let it go. Then, to cut a long story short, she suddenly turns up again five days later, wants to swap it for a bracelet, not worth as much as eight roubles. I refused, obviously. She must have read my wife's expression, so next time she came when I was out, and my wife exchanged it for the locket.

I found out about it the same day, and talked to her gently but firmly and reasonably. She was sitting on the bed, looking down at the floor, tapping her right foot on the rug (a habit she had); and she had that nasty smile on her face. So, without raising my voice at all, I calmly pointed out that the money was mine, that I had the right to live my life as I pleased, and—that when I invited her to join me in my home, I hadn't kept any secrets from her and she knew what to expect.

Suddenly she jumped up, trembling all over, and— what do you think?—she stamped her foot at me! This was a wild animal, it was a frenzy, it was a wild animal in a frenzy. I froze in amazement—I had never expected such an outburst. But I didn't lose my head, I didn't even move; I just went on in the same calm voice, telling her straight out that from that moment on I was removing her from any involvement in my work. She laughed in my face and left the apartment.

But the fact was that she had no right to leave the apartment. She was not supposed to go anywhere without me: that was our agreement even before we were married. She came home towards evening; I didn't say a word.

Next day she went out again first thing in the morning, and the day after that too. I locked up the shop and went off to see the aunts. I had broken off with them straight after our wedding day, never inviting them to us, nor us going to them. Now it turned out she hadn't gone there. They listened to me avidly, and laughed in my face. 'Serves you right,' they said. But I'd been expecting that. Straight away I bribed the younger aunt, the spinster, with a hundred roubles, and handed her twenty-five in advance. Two days later she comes to see me. 'There's an officer here,' she says, 'name of Efimovich, an ensign, used to be a comrade of yours in the regiment. He's mixed up in this.' I was astonished. This Efimovich had done me more harm than anyone in the regiment; and a month ago, shameless as he was, he had come into the shop a couple of times, pretending to pawn things; and I remember he had been laughing with my wife. I went up to him then and told him not to dare to come back to my place, remembering what our relations had been; but I'd had no idea of anything like this, I just thought he was being insolent. But now the aunt told me that he and my wife had already arranged an assignation, and the whole thing had been set up by one of the aunts' old acquaintances, the widow Yulia Samsonovna—a colonel's widow, no less. 'That's where your wife's been going these days,' she said, 'to her place.'

I'll cut this story short. The business cost me up to three hundred roubles, but within two days we had arranged that I'd be standing in the next room, with the doors closed, to listen to my wife's first private rendezvous with Efimovich. Meanwhile, the day before, a short but unforgettable scene took place between us.

She came home towards evening, sat on the bed, gave me a mocking look and tapped her foot on the carpet. As I looked at her, I suddenly thought that all that month, or rather the last two weeks, she had been behaving quite out of character; in fact, you might say, in an opposite character. She had turned into a rebellious, aggressive creature; I can't say she was shameless, but she was unruly, on the lookout for trouble. Eager for trouble. But her meekness got in her way. When that sort of woman rebels, even if she behaves outrageously, you can always see she's forcing herself, driving herself on, but she can't manage to overcome her own modesty and bashfulness. That's why these women sometimes overplay it so blatantly that you can scarcely believe what you're seeing. Whereas a woman who's used to vice will soften her behaviour, act worse, but keep up decent appearances, to make herself look superior to you.

'Is it true you were turned out of your regiment because you were scared to fight a duel?' she asked me out of the blue, her eyes glittering as she spoke.

'Yes, it's true: the officers' verdict was to ask me to resign from the regiment. Though actually I had already handed in my papers.'

'They threw you out as a coward?'

'Yes, they sentenced me for cowardice. But I refused to fight a duel, not out of cowardice, but because I wouldn't submit to their tyrannical decision and issue a challenge when I didn't consider myself insulted. You know,'—I couldn't restrain myself—'standing up against that sort of tyranny, and accepting the consequences, takes a lot more courage than fighting any duel you like.'

I couldn't resist saying that, though it looked as if I was making excuses for myself. That was all she wanted, a fresh humiliation for me. She gave a spiteful laugh.

'And is it true that after that, you spent three years wandering the streets in Petersburg like a tramp, begging for coppers and sleeping in billiard saloons?'

'I even spent nights in the Vyazemsky house on the Haymarket. Yes, it's true; after I left the regiment, I went through a lot of shame and degradation. But not moral degradation, for I was the first to loathe what I was doing, even then. It was just that my desperate situation had shattered my mind and my will. But that's all over now . . .'

'Oh yes, now you're really someone—a financier!'

That was a dig at my pawnshop. But by now I had myself in hand again. I could see she was longing for me to come out with humiliating confessions—and I didn't give her any. Just then there was a timely ring at the door—it was a customer, and I went out to the shop to deal with him. An hour later she suddenly got dressed to go out. Stopping in front of me, she said:

'But you never told me anything about that before we were married, did you?'

I didn't answer, and she left.

So next day I was standing behind the door of that room, listening to my fate being decided; and in my pocket I had a revolver. She was dressed up, sitting behind the desk, and Efimovich was showing off to her. And it turned out (I say it with pride) exactly the way I had felt and assumed it would, although I wasn't aware of having felt it or assumed it. I don't know if I'm making myself clear.

This is what happened. I listened for an hour, I was present for an hour at a duel between a noble, exalted woman and a worldly, lecherous, dull-witted brute with the soul of a worm. And how, I wondered in astonishment, could this naïve, meek, reticent creature have known all that she did? The wittiest author of a society comedy could never have created this scene of mockery, innocent laughter and the saintly contempt of virtue in the face of vice. How brilliant were her words and her little expressions, how quick-witted her lightning ripostes, how just her condemnation! And at the same time, such maidenly simplicity. She laughed in his face at his declarations of love, his gesticulations and his propositions.

He had come straight to the point, coarsely, not expecting any resistance; and now he was utterly deflated. At first I might have suspected that she was just being flirtatious—'the flirtatiousness of a depraved but clever coquette, to command a better price'. But no—the truth shone out from her like the sun, there was no doubt about it. It was only her hatred of me, impulsive and assumed, that had led this inexperienced girl to agree to this assignation. But the moment it became serious, her eyes were opened. She had been desperately keen to insult me in any way she could; but having brought herself to take this sordid step, she couldn't bear the mess of it. Could she, sinless and pure, with an ideal in her heart, ever have let herself be seduced by Efimovich, or any other society buck? Far from it—he just made her laugh. All the honesty in her indignant soul rose up and moved her to sarcasm. I repeat, by the end this buffoon had completely collapsed, sitting with a scowl on his face and barely saying a word; I was even afraid he might insult her just to get his mean revenge. And once more I repeat: to my credit, I heard that whole scene almost without surprise. I felt that nothing about it was unfamiliar. I had gone there almost on purpose to meet it, without believing anything at all, anything said against her—though I did have my revolver in my pocket. That's the truth! Could I ever have imagined her different? Why did I love her, why did I value her, why had I married her? Oh, of course, I knew only too well how much she hated me then; but I also knew how guiltless she was. I abruptly cut the scene short by opening the door. Efimovich leapt to his feet, I took her by the hand and asked her to come home with me. Efimovich pulled himself together and burst into a ringing peal of laughter.

'Oh, I've nothing to say against the sacred rights of matrimony! Take her away, take her away! You know what,' he called after me, 'although no decent man could fight you, yet out of respect to your lady, I'm at your service ... That is, if you're prepared to risk it ...'

'Listen to that!' I said, stopping her in the doorway for a second.

After that we didn't exchange a word all the way home. I led her by the hand and she didn't resist. In fact she was terribly impressed—but only till we got home. Once we were there, she sat down on a chair and stared at me. She was extraordinarily pale, and although her lips had instantly taken on a mocking smile, yet she was looking at me with stern, solemn defiance. I believe that for the first few minutes she had been seriously convinced that I was going to shoot her with the revolver. But I silently took the revolver out of my pocket and laid it on the table. She looked at me and the revolver. (Please note: she already knew this revolver. I had acquired it and loaded it when I first opened my shop. At that time I had decided not to keep huge dogs, or a burly manservant, as Moser does, for instance. When visitors come, my cook opens the door to them. But in our trade, a man can't do without some kind of self-defence, and I had chosen a loaded revolver. When she first started living in my house, she was very interested in the revolver, asked me a lot about it, and I even explained its mechanism and how to fire it. I had also once persuaded her to fire at a target. Please note all this.)

I took no notice of her frightened look, but lay down on my bed, half undressed. I was worn out—it was almost eleven by now. She went on sitting in the same place without stirring, for about an hour; then she put out the candle and lay down, also without undressing, on the sofa by the wall. This was the first time she had not come to bed with me—note that too . . .

VI. A Terrible Memory

Now for a terrible memory . . .

When I woke the next morning, sometime after seven I think, it was nearly broad daylight. I was fully conscious as soon as I woke, and opened my eyes at once. She was standing by the table, holding the revolver. She didn't notice that I had woken and was watching her. And suddenly I saw her moving towards me, with the revolver in her hand. Instantly I shut my eyes and pretended to be fast asleep.

She reached the bed and stood over me. I could hear everything; a dead silence had descended, but I could hear the very silence. Then there was a convulsive movement—and suddenly I couldn't restrain myself, and I couldn't stop myself opening my eyes. She was staring straight at me, looking me in the eyes, and the revolver was at my temple. Our eyes met. But that lasted no more than an instant. I forced myself to shut my eyes, and at that same moment I resolved with all my willpower not to make another move, nor open my eyes again, no matter what awaited me.

Sometimes it really does happen that a person who is fast asleep suddenly opens his eyes, even raises his head for a second and looks round the room, only to lose consciousness a moment later, let his head fall back on the pillow and go back to sleep, remembering nothing afterwards. When I met her eyes and felt the revolver at my temple, and then closed my eyes again and lay motionless, as though in a deep sleep—she might easily have imagined that I really was asleep and had seen nothing; for it was most unlikely that, having seen what I saw, I should have closed my eyes again at such a moment.

Yes, unlikely indeed. But she still might have guessed the truth. That thought, too, flashed through my mind at that very instant. Oh, what a whirlwind of thoughts and sensations rushed through my mind in less than the blink of an eye—hail to the electric speed of human thought! In a moment like that, so I felt, if she had guessed the truth, known that I wasn't asleep, I should already have crushed her by my willingness to accept death; and her hand might have trembled. Her resolve of a moment before might have been shattered by this new and overwhelming realization. They say that people standing at a great height are tempted to hurl themselves into the void. Many suicides and murders, I think, may have been committed merely because a person already had the revolver in his hands. For there's an abyss here too, a forty-five degree slope that you can't fail to slip down; there's something irresistible drawing you on to press the trigger. But if she was aware that I had seen everything, knew everything, and was silently awaiting death at her hands, that might have held her back on this slope.

The silence went on, and suddenly I felt, on my temple next to my hairline, the cold touch of iron. You'll wonder—was I confidently expecting to survive? I'll answer you as God is my judge: I had no such expectation, not more than one chance in a hundred. So why was I accepting death? Let me ask in my turn: what use was life to me, when the person I adored had raised a revolver against me? Besides which, I knew with all the strength of my being that a battle was raging between us in that same instant, a dreadful life-and-death duel, a duel fought by that very coward of the day before, thrown out by his comrades for coward-ice. I knew it, and she knew it, if she had only guessed the truth—that I wasn't asleep.

Maybe that didn't happen; perhaps I didn't think that at the time; but it must have happened, even without my thinking it, because I have done nothing but think about it every hour of my life since then.

But you'll ask me another question: why didn't I save her from this inhuman act? Oh, that's a question I have asked myself a thousand times since—whenever I have remembered that second, with a shiver down my spine. But my soul was in dark despair then; I was doomed, I myself was doomed, so how could I save anyone else? And how can you know whether I would have even wanted to save anyone then? Who can know what I might have felt at the time?

But my conscious mind was seething; the seconds passed, in that dead silence; still she stood over me—and suddenly I shuddered with hope! Straight away I opened my eyes. She had left the room. I got up off the bed. I had won—and she was defeated for ever!

I went out to the samovar. We always had the samovar brought to the main room, and it was always she who poured the tea. I sat down at the table without a word and accepted my cup of tea from her. Some five minutes later, I looked at her. She was dreadfully pale, paler even than the day before, and she was looking at me. And suddenly—and suddenly, seeing me looking at her, she gave a pale smile with her pale lips, with a timid question in her eyes. 'So she's still not sure, she's still wondering—does he know or doesn't he, did he see me or not?' I looked away, indifferently. After tea I locked up the shop, went to the market and bought an iron bedstead and some screens. When I came home, I had the bed placed in the main room, surrounded by screens. That was her bed, but I didn't say a word to her. And she understood, without a word, just from that bed, that I had 'seen everything, and knew everything'; there was no longer any doubt. That night, I left my revolver on the table as usual. That night, she lay down in her new bed. The marriage was broken; she was 'defeated, but not forgiven'. That night, she grew delirious, and by next morning she had a high fever. She kept to her bed for six weeks.

CHAPTER TWO

I. The Dream of Pride

Lukerya has just announced that she won't go on living here: as soon as her lady is buried, she's leaving. I knelt down and prayed for five minutes—I wanted to pray for an hour, but I kept thinking and thinking, and all my thoughts were sick ones, and I've a sick headache—what's the good of praying?—nothing but sin! Another strange thing is that I'm not sleepy. In great grief, in too great grief, after the first and the worst outbursts are over, one always wants to sleep. They say that condemned men sleep particularly soundly on their last night. And that's natural, that's how it has to be, otherwise their strength would fail them . . . I lay down on the sofa, but I couldn't sleep.

. . . For the six weeks of her illness, we cared for her day and night, Lukerya and I, with a trained nurse I had hired from the hospital. I spared no expense, in fact I even wanted to spend money on her. I called in Doctor Schroeder, and paid him ten roubles a visit. When she recovered consciousness, I mostly kept out of her way. But what's the point of describing what happened? When she was properly on her feet again, she sat quietly in my room without saying a word, at a

special table I had bought for her about that time . . .
Yes, it's true, we never spoke—I mean, we did start to
speak later, but just everyday things. Of course I made
sure never to talk too freely, but I noticed quite clearly
that she too seemed glad not to have to say a word
more than she needed. That struck me as quite natural on her part. 'She's too shaken, and too defeated,' I
thought, 'and of course she has to be allowed to forget,
and get used to it all.' And so we went on not talking;
but all the time, in my mind, I was preparing myself
for the future. I thought she was doing the same, and I
was terribly curious, always trying to guess: 'What
exactly is she thinking to herself right now?'

Another thing: oh, of course, no one can know
what I went through, moaning over her when she was
ill. But I kept my moans to myself, stifling them in my
heart, even hiding them from Lukerya. I couldn't
imagine, I couldn't even conceive of her dying without
knowing the whole truth. When she was out of danger
and beginning to recover, I remember that I quickly
calmed down completely. What's more, I resolved to
postpone our future life for as long as possible, and to
leave everything as it was for the time being. Yes, that
was when something strange and peculiar happened
to me—I can't find another word for it: I had
triumphed, and just the awareness of that was enough

for me. The whole winter passed like that. Oh, I was pleased as never before, and that lasted all winter.

You see: this terrible thing had happened to me, which had been weighing on me day by day and hour by hour, right up to the catastrophe with my wife; I mean the loss of my reputation, and my expulsion from the regiment. In a word: I had been brutally wronged. It's true that my fellow officers disliked me for my difficult character—and perhaps my ridiculous character too; for surely it often happens that what you yourself revere, cherish and honour, strikes most of your comrades as ridiculous for some reason. Oh, I was disliked even at school. I've always been disliked everywhere. Even Lukerya can't bring herself to like me. And although the incident in my regiment was caused by dislike of me, it undoubtedly came about by accident. I say this because there's nothing so hurtful and unbearable as to perish through a chance event, something that might have happened or not happened, an unfortunate combination of circumstances that might have blown over like a cloud. For an intelligent person, that's degrading. This is what happened.

At the theatre, during the interval, I had gone out to the buffet. A hussar called A—v came in and addressed two of his fellow hussars in a loud voice, in front of all the officers and everyone around, telling them that Captain Bezumtsev of our regiment had just caused a scandalous scene out in the corridor, and that 'he seems to be drunk'. The conversation went no further, and it was all a mistake, since Captain Bezumtsev wasn't drunk and the scandal hadn't actually been a scandal at all. The hussars started talking about something else, and that was the end of the matter, except that next day the story reached our regiment, and at once people pointed out that the only member of our regiment present in the buffet had been myself, and when Hussar A—v started casting aspersions on Captain Bezumtsev, I had not approached him and silenced him with a rebuke. But why should I have done? If he had something against Bezumtsev, that was their private business, and why should I have interfered? But now my fellow officers began to say that it wasn't a private matter at all, it involved the regiment too, and as I was the only officer of our regiment present, what I had done had demonstrated to all the officers and civilians in the buffet that certain officers in our regiment were not too ticklish about their own honour and that of the regiment. I couldn't accept that view. They told me that I could still put everything right if I was willing, even now, late as it was, to demand a formal explanation from A—v. I wasn't willing to do that, and in my irritation I refused haughtily. Then I handed in my resignation straight away; that's the whole story. I came out proud, but crushed in spirit. My will and my intellect had suffered a blow. And just then it happened that my sister's husband in Moscow squandered the whole of our little fortune, including my share—a tiny share, but now I was left on the street without a penny. I could have gone into private employment, but I didn't; after my splendid uniform, I couldn't have borne to take some job on the railways. So—if I had to be shamed, I'd be shamed, if I had to be disgraced, I'd be disgraced, if I had to suffer degradation, I'd suffer it, and the worse my degradation, the better; that was my choice. There followed three years of dark memories, even including the Vyazemsky house. Then, a year and a half ago, a rich old lady died in Moscow: she was my godmother, and among her other legacies she unexpectedly left me three thousand in her will. I thought it over, and at once made up my mind what to do. I decided to open a pawnshop, with no apology to anyone. Some money, a little place of my own, and a new life, far away from all my old memories: that was the plan. But my dark past, my ruined reputation, the irretrievable loss of my honour—they all weighed on me, every hour and every minute of the day. Then I got married. Whether that came about by chance or not, I don't know. But when I brought her into my house, I thought I was bringing a friend—and I needed a friend so badly! But I could see very clearly that a friend had to be prepared, schooled, even won over. Could I have explained anything at all, straight off, to this sixteen-year-old girl with all her preconceived ideas? In particular, how could I have convinced her— but for the lucky accident of that dreadful catastrophe with the revolver—that I was no coward, and that I had been unfairly accused by my regiment? So the catastrophe came in the nick of time. When I stood the test of the revolver, I avenged myself on my whole dark past. And although no one else found out about it, she did, and that was all I needed, for she herself was everything to me, my whole hope for the future, or so I dreamt! She was the only person I was making ready for myself, I needed no one else—and now she had found out everything. At least she had found out that she had been too quick to join forces with my enemies. That thought enchanted me. In her eyes, I could not be a villain any more, but at worst just an odd fellow; and after all that had happened, even that thought didn't displease me that much. Being odd is no vice; on the contrary, some females find it intriguing. In short, I purposely put off a full explanation of the truth. What had already happened was enough, and more than enough, for my peace of mind. There were already too many pictures, too many thoughts, to fill my dreams. That was my trouble—I was a dreamer; all I needed was material for my dreams. As for her—I thought she could wait.

The whole winter went by like that—with us both seemingly waiting for something. I loved to steal a glance at her as she sat at her table. She would be stitching, mending the linen, and sometimes in the evenings she might read a book taken from my book-case. The choice of books there must also have done me some credit. She almost never went out. After dinner, before dusk fell, I would take her for a walk to get some exercise, but it would not be in total silence as before. I would try to pretend that we weren't walking in silence, that we were having a friendly conversation; but as I've said, we both avoided saying much. I did that on purpose; I thought it was essential to 'give her time'. Of course it was strange that it never once occurred to me, all winter long, that I loved to steal furtive looks at her—but never once in all that time did I ever catch her casting a single glance at me! I thought that she was just being timid. She had such a meek, shy look, such a helpless look, after her illness. 'No, better wait,' I thought—'and she'll suddenly come to you of her own accord . . .'

That thought appealed to me beyond anything. Let me just add this: sometimes I worked myself up almost on purpose, convincing myself that I felt injured by her. Those episodes would last some time. But my resentment could never ripen or take root in my heart. I myself felt that this was, in a way, only a game. Even when I broke off our marriage and bought the bed and the screens, I could never, never look on her as a criminal. Not because I didn't take her crime seriously—but because from the very first day, even before I bought the bed, I intended to forgive her completely. That was a piece of strange behaviour on my part, for I am strict in moral matters. But in my eyes she was so defeated, so humbled, so crushed, that I sometimes felt agonizingly sorry for her—though at the same time I sometimes really enjoyed the idea of her humiliation. I enjoyed the sense of inequality between us . . .

It so happened that I did several good deeds that winter. I excused two debts, and gave money to one poor woman without requiring a pledge in return. And I told my wife nothing about those acts: I hadn't done them in order for her to find out. But the woman herself came to thank me, almost falling on her knees. So it all came out; and I thought my wife was really pleased when she found out about the woman.

But spring was coming, it was halfway through April, the double windows were taken out, and the sun shone its bright beams into our silent rooms. Yet there seemed to be a veil hanging before my eyes, casting blindness on my mind. A terrible, fateful veil! How did this veil come to fall from my eyes, so that I suddenly saw and understood everything? Was it chance, or had the hour come, or had some sunray fired up a thought, a realization, in my sluggish mind? No, it was no thought and no realization; it was a nerve that suddenly awoke, a nerve that had long lain numb and now began to vibrate, and came alive, and illuminated my whole torpid soul and its diabolical pride. I almost leapt up from my seat then—it was so sudden, so unexpected. It happened in the early evening, around five o'clock, after dinner . . .

II. The Veil Suddenly Falls

Just two words before I start. A month or so ago I had noticed her being strangely pensive—not just silent, but pensive. That, too, was something I noticed suddenly. At the time, she was sitting at her work, bending over her sewing, and didn't notice me looking at her. And I realized that she had grown so thin, so wasted, and her face was pale, and her lips were white;

all these things, along with her pensiveness, struck me forcibly in that moment. I had already heard her quiet, dry cough, especially at night. Now I got up and went straight out to ask Schroeder to visit, without saying a word to her.

Schroeder came next day. She was very surprised, looking from Schroeder to me in turn.

'But I'm perfectly well,' she said, with a vague smile.

Schroeder didn't spend long examining her (these medical types can be condescending and offhand); he just took me next door and told me that this was the after-effect of her illness, and that when spring came it wouldn't be a bad idea to go away to the seaside, or if that wasn't possible, then just to go to the country for a bit. In fact he didn't tell me anything to the point, except that she had a weakness or something of the kind. When Schroeder had gone, she suddenly gave me a terribly serious look and repeated:

'I'm quite, quite well.'

But as soon as she had said that, she blushed, apparently from shame. Apparently it was shame. Oh, now I understand—she was ashamed that I was still her husband, still looking after her like a real husband. But at the time I didn't realize that, and put her blush down to her humility. (That veil!)

So then, a month later, sometime after four in the afternoon on a bright, sunny April day, I was sitting at the shop counter doing the accounts. Suddenly I heard her, in our room, sitting sewing at her table and softly, softly . . . starting to sing. This was something so new, it made an overpowering impression on me; and to this day I don't understand it. Up till then I had scarcely ever heard her sing, except in our very first days together, when I brought her into my home and we could still have fun together, firing the revolver at a target. In those days she had a fairly strong, resonant voice; it wasn't quite true, but was very sweet and healthy. But now her singing was so faint—oh, not that it was mournful (she was singing some sort of romance), but it sounded as if her voice had somehow cracked or broken, as if that little voice of hers couldn't cope—as if the song itself was sick. She was singing to herself, and then she abruptly broke off and got up—such a pitiful little voice, breaking off in such a sorry way . . . She coughed, and then, very quietly, almost inaudibly, began singing again . . .

People will find my emotion ridiculous—no one will ever understand why I was so moved! No, I wasn't sorry for her yet: this was something quite different. At first, at least for the first few minutes, I was just aston- ished, all at once, filled with a feeling of surprise, so strange, so strange and terrible, morbid, almost vindictive: 'Singing—in my presence! Can she have forgotten about me?'

Quite shattered, I stayed where I was; then I quickly stood up, took my hat and got ready to go out, without thinking what I was doing. At least, I don't know why or where I was going. Lukerya brought me my coat.

'She sings, does she?' I found myself asking her. She didn't understand me, and gave me a long, puzzled stare. True, I wasn't making myself clear.

'Is this the first time she's been singing?'

'No, she sometimes sings when you're out,' Lukerya replied.

I remember everything. I went downstairs and out to the street, and walked off, just following my nose. When I got to the corner, I began staring vacantly around. People walked past, jostling me, but I didn't feel them. I called a cab and told the driver to take me to the Police Bridge, I've no idea why. Then I suddenly changed my mind and gave him twenty kopeks: 'That's for your trouble,' I said, with a pointless laugh. But all at once my heart was filled with a sort of rapture.

I turned back and quickened my steps. At a stroke, that cracked, pitiful, broken note was ringing in my heart again. I fought for breath. The veil was falling,

falling from my eyes! When she started singing in my presence, it meant she had forgotten about me—that was the clear and terrible thing. My heart could feel it. But the rapture shone out in my soul, and overcame my terror.

O, the irony of fate! All winter long my soul had known nothing else, could have known nothing else but this same rapture—but where had I been, myself, all winter? Had I been with my own soul then? I ran upstairs in great haste; I don't know if I came in timidly or not. All I remember is that the whole floor seemed to be rocking, I felt as if I was floating down a river. I came into the room; she was sitting in the same place, still sewing, with her head bent over her work, but not singing any more. She cast an incurious, passing glance at me, but it wasn't really a glance, more the kind of everyday, indifferent movement one makes when someone enters a room.

I went straight over to her and sat down on a chair, right close up to her, like a madman. She gave me a quick look, as if she was frightened; I took her hand; I don't remember what I said to her, or rather what I wanted to say, because I couldn't even talk properly. My voice was cracking, it wouldn't obey me; and I didn't even know what to say, I was just panting for breath.

'Let's talk ... you know ... say something!' I babbled senselessly—oh, was there any place for sense just then? She gave another start and recoiled in real alarm, staring at my face. But suddenly an expression of stern astonishment came into her eyes. Yes, astonishment—and stern, too. She was staring at me, wide-eyed. And her sternness, her stern astonishment, floored me instantly. 'So you still want love? Love?' her astonished expression seemed to say, though she herself said not a word. But I read it all, all of it. Everything within me shuddered, and I simply collapsed at her feet. Yes, I fell at her feet. She jumped up at once, but I held on to both her hands with all my might.

And I completely understood my despair, oh, I understood it! But, would you believe it, that rapture surged up in my heart so irrepressibly, I thought I should die. I kissed her feet in an ecstasy of happiness. Yes, happiness, measureless and endless, even as I realized the hopelessness of my despair. I was weeping, saying words, but quite incoherent. She ceased to be frightened and astonished, and suddenly became apprehensive, filled with some important question, and she gave me a strange look, a wild look—she wanted to understand something quickly, and she smiled. She was dreadfully ashamed that I was kissing her feet, and drew them back, but I at once kissed the place on the floor where her foot had been. She saw me do it, and began laughing with embarrassment (you know how it happens, when a person laughs with embarrassment). She was becoming hysterical, I could see that—her hands were shaking—but I didn't think about that, I just kept mumbling that I loved her, that I wouldn't get up from the floor, 'let me kiss your dress . . . let me worship you like this all your life . . .' I don't know, I don't remember—but suddenly she burst out sobbing and shaking, and lapsed into a dreadful fit of hysterics. I had petrified her.

I carried her over to the bed. When her attack passed off, she sat on the edge of the bed with a fearfully washed-out look, seized hold of my hands and begged me to calm down. 'Do stop, don't torment yourself, keep calm!' she said—and started crying once more. All that evening I never left her side. I kept telling her I'd take her to Boulogne, to bathe in the sea, right now, straight away, in two weeks; that her little voice was so cracked, I had heard it earlier on; that I'd close down the pawnshop, sell it to Dobronravov, and we'd start afresh, and, above all, off to Boulogne, to Boulogne! She listened to all this and it frightened her. She grew more and more afraid. But that wasn't what mattered most to me—what mattered most was that I had this more and more irresistible urge to lie down again at her feet, and kiss the ground she stood on, and kiss it again, and worship her—and 'I'll never ask anything of you again, anything at all,' I kept repeating on and on, 'don't answer me, take no notice of me whatever, just let me watch you from my corner, turn me into your thing, your little puppy . . .' And she was weeping.

'I was thinking you'd let me go on like that,' she burst out without meaning to—so unconsciously that perhaps she wasn't even aware of saying it; although— oh, that was the most important and fateful thing she had said that evening, and the one I understood best: it was like the slash of a knife across my heart! It explained everything to me, everything, but so long as she was near me, so long as I had her before my eyes, my hope remained irrepressible, and I was terribly happy. Oh, I had exhausted her dreadfully that evening, and I realized it, but I kept on thinking that I was going to change everything at once. In the end, by nightfall, she was wiped out, and I persuaded her to go to sleep. And she fell asleep instantly, sound asleep. I was expecting her to become delirious, and she did, but only slightly. I got up every minute, all night long, and went in quietly in my slippers to look at her. And I wrung my hands over her, as I gazed at this sick creature on her wretched bed, that iron bedstead I had bought for her for three roubles. I knelt down beside her as she slept, but did not dare kiss her feet (without her consent!). I began praying to God, but leapt up again. Lukerya was watching me—she kept coming out of the kitchen to see. I went and told her to go to bed, and said that tomorrow 'everything would be quite different'.

And I believed it—blindly, insanely, dreadfully. O the rapture, the rapture that filled me to overflowing! All I wanted was for the day to come. The main thing was, I didn't believe that anything bad would happen, in spite of the symptoms. I had not entirely regained my reason yet, though the veil had fallen from my eyes; and it was a long, long time before my reason returned—oh, not till today, till this very day! And how could it, how could it have returned at the time: for she was still alive then, she was right there in front of me, and I in front of her. 'She'll wake up tomorrow, and I'll tell her all this, and she'll see it all.' That was the way I reasoned then, simply and clearly, and hence my rapture! The main thing for me was this trip to Boulogne. For some reason I kept thinking that Boulogne was everything, that Boulogne contained something final. 'To Boulogne, to Boulogne!' I waited desperately for the morning.

III. I Understand All Too Well

And this was only a few days ago, five days, not more than five days, just last Tuesday! No, no, if only she had waited just a little longer, just the tiniest bit longer—I would have blown away the darkness! Had she really not calmed down? The very next day she listened to me with a smile, despite her confusion . . . The main thing was that all that time, in all those five days, there was some confusion in her mind, some embarrassment. And she was frightened, too, very frightened. I don't dispute that, I won't contradict it like a madman: yes, she was frightened, but after all, how could she not have been? We had become strangers to one another so long ago, become so unused to each other, and suddenly all this . . . But I wasn't concerned with her fear, something new was shining out now! . . It's true, it's definitely true that I made a mistake. Perhaps, in fact, there were many mistakes. Next morning, as soon as we woke up, straight away in the early morning (that was on Wednesday), right from the start I made a mistake: I made her my friend. I was in a hurry, far too much of a hurry, but a confession was needed, was essential—and more than a confession! I didn't even hide from her what I had been hiding from myself all my life. I told her straight out that all I had done, all that winter, was to live in the certainty that she loved me. I explained that opening my pawnshop was merely the degradation of my will and my mind, my own way of punishing and also exalting myself. I explained to her that back then, in the theatre buffet, I really had acted out of cowardice, because of my character, my self-doubt. I had been overcome by my surroundings, in that buffet; I was worried about how I would look, and wouldn't I seem foolish . . . I wasn't frightened of a duel, I was frightened of looking a fool. And after that I never wanted to own up, and tormented everyone, and tormented her too, and had only married her in order to torment her because of it. And she took me by the hands and begged me to stop. 'You're exaggerating . . . you're tormenting yourself . . .', and then there were more tears, and again she almost fell into a fit of hysterics! She kept asking me to stop saying all this, and stop going over it.

I took no notice, or not much notice, of her pleading: it would soon be spring, Boulogne! The sun would be shining there, our new sun, that was all I could repeat! I shut up the shop, and handed the business over to Dobronravov. I abruptly suggested to her that we could give all our money to the poor, except for the three thousand from my godmother, which we'd use to travel to Boulogne, and after that we'd come back home and start a new life of proper work. And that's what we decided to do, because she didn't say anything . . . she just smiled. And I believe she smiled more out of delicacy, so as not to upset me. I could see, you know, that I was a burden to her; don't think that I was so stupid, or so selfish, as not to see that. I saw everything, everything down to the last detail, I saw it and knew it better than anyone; all my despair was there in full view.

I told her all about myself, and about her. And about Lukerya. I told her that I had been in tears . . . Oh, but I did change the subject, I did try not to mention certain subjects at all. And truly, she did liven up, once or twice—I remember that, I do! Why do you say that I wasn't seeing what was staring me in the face? If only this hadn't happened, everything would have come back to life again. After all, she had told me herself, only the day before yesterday, when we were talking about reading and what she had read this winter—she had laughed as she remembered the scene in *Gil Blas* with the Archbishop of Granada. What sweet, childish laughter, just like before, when she was engaged to me (just for one instant! one instant!); how glad I was! Actually I was terribly struck by that memory of the Archbishop: for didn't it mean that this winter, sitting at home, she had found so much tranquillity of mind, so much happiness, that she could laugh at that masterpiece? That meant that she really had begun to regain her peace of mind, she really had begun to believe that I'd let her go on like that. 'I thought you'd let me go on like this'—that was what she had said, on that Tuesday. Oh, the thoughts of a ten-year-old girl! And she had believed, she truly had, that everything really would stay like that: with her sitting at her own table, and me at mine, and both of us like that, until we were sixty. And suddenly— here I come, a husband, and the husband needs love! Oh the delusion, oh my blindness!

Another mistake was my looking at her with rapture. I should have controlled myself; my rapture frightened her. But I did control myself, I did—I stopped kissing her feet. Not once did I give any sign of . . . well, of being her husband—oh, that thought never even crossed my mind, all I did was worship her! But I couldn't keep completely silent, could I?—I couldn't just not speak at all! I went and told her that I delighted in her conversation, and regarded her as far, far more educated and cultured than I was. She blushed deeply, quite embarrassed, and said that I was exaggerating. And at that point I was so stupid—I couldn't control myself, and told her how enraptured I had been when I was standing behind the door listen-ing to her battle, the battle of innocence against that wretch, and how I had delighted in her intelligence, her sparkling wit, alongside her childlike simplicity. She gave a sort of shudder all over her body, muttered once more that I was exaggerating, but suddenly her whole face darkened, she hid it in her hands and began sobbing . . . Well, then I couldn't hold out, I fell to the floor before her again, and started kissing her feet again, and again it all ended in a fit of hysterics, just like Tuesday. That was yesterday evening, and next morning . . . Next morning?! You madman, that morning was today, just now, only just now!

Listen to me, and try to understand: when we met this morning by the samovar (after yesterday's hyster-ics), she actually startled me with her calmness—that's really how it was! Meanwhile I had spent the whole night shaking with fear because of what had happened the evening before. And abruptly she came up to me, stood in front of me, clasped her hands together (just now, this was—just now!) and told me that she was a criminal, and she knew that, and that her crime had tormented her all winter, and was still tormenting her now . . . and that she treasured my generosity, and . . . 'I shall be your faithful wife, I shall respect you . . .' At which point I sprang to my feet and embraced her like a madman! I was kissing her, kissing her face, kissing her on the lips as a husband does, for the first time after a long separation. But oh why, why did I go out just then—for no more than two hours . . . our passports for abroad . . . Oh God, just five minutes, if only I had come back just five minutes earlier! . . And that crowd in our gateway, everybody looking at me . . . Oh God!

Lukerya says (oh, I'll never let Lukerya go now, not for anything, she knows everything, she's been here all winter, she'll tell me all about it), she says that after I had left the house, and only some twenty minutes before I came back—she went into our room to ask the lady something, I don't remember what, and saw that she had taken out her icon (that same icon of the Mother of God), and it was standing on the table in front of her, and the lady seemed to be praying to it just then. 'What is it, madam?'—'Nothing, Lukerya, you can go now . . . Wait a moment, Lukerya,' and she went up to her and kissed her. 'Are you happy, madam?'—'Yes, Lukerya.'—'The master should have come to you long ago, to ask your pardon . . . Thank God you've made your peace now.'—'Very well, Lukerya,' she says, 'go now, Lukerya,' and she gave a smile, but a strange sort of smile. So strange, that Lukerya went back ten minutes later, to have a look at her. 'And she's standing there by the wall, right next to the window, leaning her hand on the wall, pressing her head against her hand, and she's standing like that, thinking. And she's so deep in her thoughts, she didn't even notice me standing there watching her from the other room. And I see her, she seems to be smiling; she's standing, thinking and smiling. I looked at her, and turned quietly away and went out, and I'm thinking to myself, and suddenly I hear the window being opened. I went straight back to tell her, "It's cold, madam, you don't want to catch a chill," and suddenly I see, she's got up on the windowsill and she's standing there, straight upright, in the open window, with her back to me, and she's holding the icon in her hands. My heart just sank, I called out, "Madam, madam!"— She heard me, made a move to turn round to me, but she didn't turn, she took a step forward, pressed the icon to her breast—and jumped out of the window!'

All I remember is that when I came back through the gates, she was still warm. The thing was, they were all looking at me. First they were shouting, but then they all suddenly stopped, and everyone in front of me moved aside, and . . . and she's lying there with the icon. I remember, through a sort of blackness—I went silently up to her, and took a long look at her, and everyone gathered round and they were saying something to me. Lukerya was there, but I didn't see her. They tell me she was talking to me. All I remember is one tradesman, who kept yelling at me, 'There was a handful of blood came out of her mouth, just a handful, a handful!' and pointed to the blood on a stone right there. I think I touched the blood with my finger, I smeared my finger, and I looked at the finger (that I remember), and he keeps going on, 'a handful, just a handful!'

'What do you mean, a handful?' I screamed at the top of my voice, so they tell me; and I raised my arms and hurled myself at him ... 'Oh, how unspeakable, how unspeakable! Oh, the delusion! Unbelievable! Impossible!'

IV. *Just Five Minutes Too Late*

Isn't that right? Wasn't it incredible? Could one really say it was possible? Why did this woman die—what for?

Oh, believe me, I do understand; but what she died for, that's still a question. Got frightened of my love, asked herself seriously: whether to accept me or not; and couldn't bear the question, and preferred to die. I know, I know, no use racking my brains over it: she'd made too many promises, got frightened that she wouldn't be able to keep them—that's obvious. Some things about it are absolutely dreadful.

I mean—what did she die for?—that question still stands. It batters me, batters my brain. I'd have let things go on like that, if that was what she wanted. But she didn't believe it, that's what it was! No, no, I'm getting it wrong, it wasn't that at all. It was just that with me, things had to be honest: if it was love, then love with all her heart, not the way she would have loved that shopkeeper. And since she was too chaste, too pure, to accept the sort of love the shopkeeper would have needed, she didn't want to deceive me. She didn't want to deceive me with half-love, or quarter-love, passing it off as love. Too honest, that's what it was! And I had wanted to graft broadmindedness into her heart, remember? An odd idea.

A very curious thought: did she respect me? I don't know whether she despised me or not. I don't think she did. It's terribly strange: why did it never occur to me, all winter long, that she despised me? I was utterly convinced of the contrary, right up to the very moment when she looked at me with stern astonishment. Stern it was. Then I realized in an instant that she despised me. Understood it once for all, for ever! Oh, let her have despised me, let her despise me all her life long—but let her be alive, alive! Just a short time ago she was still walking and talking. I simply can't understand how she can have thrown herself out of the window! And how could I have conceived of it, even five minutes before? I called Lukerya. I shan't let Lukerya go now, not for anything, no, not for anything!

Oh, we could still have sorted everything out. We had just got terribly unused to each other over the winter, but even so, couldn't we have got used to each other again? Why, oh why, couldn't we have come together and started a new life again? I'm generous-hearted, so's she—so there's a point where we could have met! Just a few more words, another couple of days, no more, and she'd have understood everything.

What hurts most is that all this happened by chance—simple, brutal, accidental chance. How that hurts! Five minutes, no more, a mere little five minutes too late! If I'd come just five minutes earlier—then the moment would have passed, passed over like a cloud, and it would never have occurred to her after that. And it would have ended with her understanding everything. But now—those empty rooms once more, and I'm back on my own. Listen to the clock ticking, it doesn't care, it has no pity. There's no one—that's the misery of it!

I pace around, I keep pacing around. I know, I know, don't tell me—you think it's funny, me complaining about an accidental chance and five minutes? But it's obvious, isn't it? Just consider: she didn't even leave a note to say 'Don't blame anyone for my death', the way everyone does. Surely she could have realized that it might even have got Lukerya into trouble—'She was with her, she must have given her a push.' They might well have hauled her off, innocent though she was, but for those four people outside, who saw her out of their windows or from the yard, standing with the icon in her hands and jumping out of her own accord. But that was a chance too, those people standing there and seeing her. No, all that just happened in an instant, an unaccountable instant. A sudden whim! So what if she was praying before the icon? That doesn't mean she was facing death. That whole moment might have lasted no more than ten minutes or so, perhaps, that whole decision of hers—just for the time while she was standing by the wall, resting her head in her hand, and smiling. The idea flew into her head, and whirled around, and—she couldn't resist it.

Say what you like, there was obviously some misunderstanding. She could still have lived with me. Or perhaps she was anaemic? Simple anaemia, exhaustion of her vital energy? She'd got tired over the winter, that's what . . .

Too late!!!

How thin she is in her coffin, how sharp her little nose is! Her eyelashes lying like little arrows. And the way she fell—nothing crushed, nothing broken! Nothing but that little 'handful of blood'. Meaning a dessert-spoonful. Internal injury. A strange thought: what if it were possible not to bury her? Because if they take her away, then . . . oh no, they can't possibly take her away! Oh, of course I know they have to take her away, I'm not insane, I'm not raving, not at all, on the contrary, my mind has never shone clearer—but how can it be, no one in the house again, those two rooms again, and me on my own with the pledges . . . Raving, raving, here's the raving! I wore her out, that's what!

What are your laws to me now? What use are your customs, your morals, your life, your state, your faith? Let your judge pass judgment on me, let them take me to court, to your public court, and I'll say: I admit nothing. The judge will shout 'Silence, officer!' And I'll shout back, 'Where's your power now, to force me to obey? Why should some dark, mindless force smash up the most precious thing of all? What's the sense of your laws to me now? I reject them!' Oh, I don't care!

Blind, blind! Dead, she can't hear me! You don't know what a paradise I would have made for you. I had paradise in my soul, I would have planted it for you. All right, you might not have loved me—never mind, what would it matter? Everything would have been like that, and everything would have stayed like that. You could have told me about things as a friend—and we'd have been joyful, and laughed happily together, looking into each other's eyes. And we'd have lived like that. And even if you'd loved someone else—never mind, never mind! You'd have walked with him, and laughed, and I'd have watched you from across the road . . . Oh, anything, anything, if she'd only open her eyes just once! For an instant, just one instant! to look at me, as she did this morning, when she stood before me and vowed to be a faithful wife! Oh, in one look she'd have understood everything!

Blind fate! Oh, nature! People are alone on earth—that's the dreadful thing! 'Is there a living man on the field?' cries out the Russian hero. And I, no hero, cry it out too, and no one answers. They say the sun gives life to the universe. The sun will rise, and—look at it, isn't it a corpse? Everything is dead, and the corpses are everywhere. Nothing but people, and around them—silence: that's the earth! 'People, love one another'—who said that? Whose commandment is that? The clock ticks, heartlessly, horribly. Two o'clock in the morning. Her little boots are standing by her bed, waiting for her . . . No, seriously, when they take her away tomorrow, what will become of me?

THE CROCODILE

An Extraordinary event that occurred in the Arcade

The true story of how a gentleman of a certain age and respectable appearance was swallowed alive, whole and entire, by a crocodile exhibited in the Arcade, and of what happened next.

Ohé Lambert! Où est Lambert? As-tu vu Lambert?

I

ON THE THIRTEENTH of January of this present year of 1865, at half past midday, Elena Ivanovna, the spouse of Ivan Matveich, my cultured friend and professional colleague (and in a sense also my distant relative), expressed a wish to see the crocodile exhibited in the Arcade on payment of an admission fee. Ivan Matveich already had a railway ticket in his pocket for a trip abroad (not so much for his health as to satisfy his thirst for knowledge); consequently he was officially on leave from his post, and therefore quite free that morning. He raised no objection to his wife's fervent wish; indeed, he too was burning with curiosity.

'What a splendid idea!' he said with great satisfaction. 'Let us have a look at the crocodile! Since we are taking a trip to Europe, it's not a bad idea to get to know its native population before we go.' And with these words he took his wife's arm and they went straight off to the Arcade. As a friend of the family, I went along with them as usual. I had never seen Ivan Matveich in a more convivial mood than on that memorable morning. How true it is that we never know what awaits us!

When we reached the Arcade, he at once fell into raptures over the splendour of the building; and when we came to the booth where the monster lately arrived in our capital city was being exhibited, he insisted on paying the crocodile keeper my quarter-rouble entrance fee—something he had never done before. We entered a small room to find that besides the crocodile, it also housed some of those foreign parrots they call cockatoos, not to mention a troop of monkeys in a special cage in a corner. On the left of the entrance stood a large tin bath-shaped container, covered with a tough iron mesh, with a couple of inches of water in the bottom. This shallow puddle contained a gigantic crocodile, lying there as still as a log; it seemed that our damp climate, so inhospitable to foreign visitors, had deprived it of all its faculties. At first this monster aroused no particular curiosity in any of us.

'So this is the crocodile!' quavered Elena Ivanovna in a disappointed voice. 'I thought it would be . . . different, somehow!'

She probably expected it to be made of diamonds. The crocodile's owner came over to us looking incredibly pleased with himself.

'No wonder he's pleased,' Ivan Matveich whispered to me. 'He knows that he's the only man in all Russia exhibiting a crocodile.'

I attribute this utterly pointless observation to Ivan Matveich's now being in an exceptionally good mood—for he was normally the envious type.

'I don't believe your crocodile is alive at all,' said Elena Ivanovna, piqued by the owner's unshakeable self-satisfaction and addressing him with a gracious smile intended to puncture his boorish complacency. How typical of a woman.

'O no, madam,' answered the owner in broken Russian; and immediately lifted the iron mesh half off the tank and began prodding the crocodile's head with a stick.

The sly monster gave a sign of life, slightly moving its feet and tail, lifting its snout and uttering something like a long-drawn-out snuffle.

'Come on, don't be cross, Karlchen!' said the German affectionately; his vanity was satisfied.

'How repulsive this crocodile is! It quite frightened me,' lisped Elena Ivanovna, even more coquettishly. 'I'm sure I'll dream about it now.'

'But he will not bite you in your sleep, madam,' the German gallantly assured her, and was the first to laugh at his own joke. None of us joined in.

'Come along, Semyon Semyonich,' Elena Ivanovna went on, addressing me alone. 'Let's go and look at the monkeys instead. I really love monkeys, they're so sweet . . . but that crocodile is horrible.'

'Don't worry, darling!' Ivan Matveich called after us, enjoying showing off his manly courage to his spouse. 'This somnolent denizen of the empire of the Pharaohs won't hurt us.' And he stayed behind by the tank. What was more, he began to tickle the crocodile's snout with his glove, trying—as he later admitted—to make the beast snuffle again. The owner followed Elena Ivanovna—since she was a lady—to the monkeys' cage.

So everything was going splendidly, and no one could have foreseen what happened next. Elena

Ivanovna was being quite playful and mischievous with the monkeys; she seemed very taken with them. She was squealing with delight, talking only to me, deliberately ignoring the owner, and giggling at how closely those creatures resembled her intimate friends and acquaintances. I became quite merry myself, for there was no doubt of the resemblance. The German didn't know whether or not to laugh, and ended up putting on a sulky scowl. But at that very moment a terrible—I might even say unearthly—shriek echoed through the room. I did not know what to make of it, and froze where I stood; but then I saw Elena Ivanovna screaming too. I whirled round, and what should I see! I saw— oh my God—I saw the wretched Ivan Matveich in the dreadful jaws of the crocodile, which had seized him by the waist and lifted him horizontally high in the air, while he kicked frantically with his legs. Another instant, and he was gone. But let me describe it in detail, because all this time I was standing motionless, watching the whole thing happening before my eyes, more avidly curious than I had ever been before. 'For suppose,' I thought to myself in that fateful moment, 'suppose all this had happened, not to Ivan Matveich, but to me . . . how exceedingly unpleasant I should have found it!'

But to come back to my story. The crocodile began by turning poor Ivan Matveich legs downwards between its terrible jaws. It swallowed the legs, then belched him back up a little way (at that, my friend struggled to jump out, scrabbling at the sides of the tank) and swallowed him down again, this time to above his waist. Another belch, followed by another gulp, and another. Ivan Matveich was disappearing before our eyes. At last, with one final gulp, the crocodile engulfed my cultured friend whole, leaving no trace of him at all. Looking at the crocodile's exterior, one could make out every detail of Ivan Matveich's shape, as it passed down through the monster's innards. I was about to scream again when fate played another cruel trick on us. The crocodile tensed itself, probably struggling with the huge mouthful it had swallowed, and opened its horrible jaws once more. Out came Ivan Matveich's head for one second, like a last eructation, with a look of despair on his face; his glasses toppled off his nose and fell to the bottom of the tank. It seemed as if this despairing head had reappeared only to cast one last look around, and take its leave of all earthly pleasures. But this it never managed: the crocodile gathered up its strength again, swallowed— and in an instant the head was gone, this time for ever. This appearance and disappearance of a living human head was so appalling—and yet (perhaps because the event was so rapid and unexpected, or perhaps because of the spectacles that fell off his nose) so comic at the same time, that I actually gave a sudden snort of laughter. But I realized straight away that as a family friend it was improper of me to be laughing, so I instantly turned to Elena Ivanovna and said sympathetically:

'Well, that's the end of our friend Ivan Matveich!'

I cannot begin to describe the abject distress of Elena Ivanovna throughout this whole episode. To start with, after her first shriek, she stood rooted to the spot, seemingly impassive as she watched the confused spectacle, though her eyes were starting out of her head. Then suddenly she burst out in a heartrending wail, and I seized her hands. At this point the proprietor, who had stood transfixed with horror himself at first, threw up his hands and cried out to the heavens:

'*Ach mein Krokodil, O mein allerliebster Karlchen! Mutter, Mutter, Mutter!*'

At this cry the rear door burst open and Mutter appeared, a red-faced, dishevelled old woman in a bonnet. She screamed and rushed over to her German.

Now there was an uproar. Elena Ivanovna was like a woman possessed, screeching the same words over and over again: 'Hit it! Hit it!' She ran to the proprietor and Mutter, apparently entreating them (probably in some confusion) to beat someone for some fault. Neither the proprietor nor Mutter took the slightest notice of us; both stood bellowing like calves beside the crocodile's tank.

'He is *kaputt*, now he shall bursting, because he swallowing *ganz* one official!' shrieked the proprietor.

'*Unser Karlchen, unser allerliebster Karlchen wird sterben!*' wailed Mutter.

'We orphan now, no bread to eat,' the proprietor echoed her.

'Hit it, hit it, hit it!' fulminated Elena Ivanovna, clutching the German by his coat.

'He teasing crocodile—what for your husband teasing crocodile?' shouted the German, shaking her off. 'You shall pay, if Karlchen shall bursting—*das war mein Sohn, das war mein einziger Sohn!*'

I must confess I felt terribly indignant at the sight of such egoism on the part of this German immigrant, and at the heartless attitude of his slovenly Mutter. But I was even more alarmed by the incessant screams of 'hit it, hit it!' from Elena Ivanovna; in the end I was completely riveted by her, and also quite frightened. I must make it clear here that I had completely misunderstood her strange exclamations. I had the mistaken impression that she had momentarily taken leave of her senses, and wanted to avenge the destruction of her beloved Ivan Matveich by having the crocodile thrashed with a stick, by way of compensation due to her. In fact I had entirely mistaken her meaning. In some embarrassment, I looked back at the entrance door, begging Elena Ivanovna to calm down, and most particularly to stop using the emotive words 'hit it'. Such an unenlightened demand, right here in the middle of the Arcade, surrounded as we were by cultured persons, and only a stone's throw from the very hall where Mr Lavrov might even then be delivering a public lecture—such a thing was impossible, indeed unthinkable. At any moment it might provoke angry hisses from the intelligentsia, and caricatures by Mr Stepanov. And to my horror, I was immediately proved right. There were curtains separating the crocodile room from the lobby where the quarter-rouble entrance fees were collected. These curtains suddenly parted, and a man with a moustache and beard, holding a cap in his hands, appeared on the threshold. He was leaning over forward as far as he could with the upper part of his body, while very carefully keeping his feet outside the entrance to the crocodile room so as not to have to pay the entrance fee.

'Such a reactionary wish, madam,' said the stranger, doing his best not to fall across the threshold but keep his feet planted outside, 'does no credit to your intellect, and indicates a deficiency of phosphorus in your brain. You will find yourself instantly shamed in the chronicles of progress, and in our satirical papers—'

But he never finished. As soon as the horrified proprietor realized that the man was talking inside the crocodile room without having paid for a ticket, he hurled himself furiously at this unknown progressive, punched him in the neck with first one fist and then the other, and threw him out. For an instant they both disappeared out of sight behind the curtain, and only then did I suddenly realize that all this uproar had been a fuss about nothing. Elena Ivanovna was completely guiltless. She had not had the least intention of subjecting the crocodile to a reactionary and humiliating beating with sticks, as I noted above; all she had wanted was to have it *slit*—not hit: to have its belly slit open with a knife, to release Ivan Matveich from its innards.

'How! You wanting my crocodile perish!' howled the proprietor, bursting back into the room. 'No, let your husband must first perishing, then the crocodile after! . . *Mein Vater* showing this crocodile, *mein Grossvater* showing this crocodile, *mein Sohn* shall showing this crocodile, and I shall showing this crocodile. Everybody shall showing the crocodile! I am famous in *ganz Europa*, but you not famous in *ganz Europa* and you must *eine Strafe* pay to me!'

'*Ja, ja!*' echoed the spiteful Mutter. 'We not let you go, you must *eine Strafe* pay, if Karlchen bursting!'

'In any case, there's no point slitting it open,' I added calmly, hoping to distract Elena Ivanovna and get her home as quickly as possible; 'for by now our dear Ivan Matveich is in all likelihood soaring aloft somewhere in the empyrean.'

'My friend!'—Suddenly, to our utter amazement, we heard the voice of Ivan Matveich himself. 'My friend, your best course in my view is to address yourself directly to the supervisor's office. Without the assistance of the police, the German will never see reason.'

These words were pronounced firmly and emphatically, indicating exceptional presence of mind in the speaker. At first we were so astonished that we couldn't believe our ears.

But of course we all ran over to the crocodile tank, to listen with no less veneration than incredulity to the unhappy prisoner. His voice was muffled, thin and even squeaky, as if it came from very far away. It reminded me of what happens when some joker goes into another room, covers his mouth with a pillow, and starts shouting, so that his listeners in the first room seem to be hearing two peasants calling to one another across a wilderness or a deep ravine (I had once had the pleasure of hearing such a performance at a friend's house one Christmas).

'Ivan Matveich, my dear—so you're alive!' stammered Elena Ivanovna.

'Alive and well,' said Ivan Matveich, 'and by the grace of the Almighty, swallowed without the least injury. My only anxiety is what view my superiors will take of this episode—for having obtained a permit for travel abroad, I have ended up in a crocodile, which was far from clever.'

'My dear, don't worry about being clever. The first thing to be done is to extricate you from there somehow,' interrupted Elena Ivanovna.

'Extricate!' yelled the proprietor, 'I not let you extricate my crocodile. Now the *Publikum* shall much more come here, and I shall ask *fünfzig* kopeks, and Karlchen shall stop bursting.'

'*Gott sei Dank!*' exclaimed his wife.

'They're right,' remarked Ivan Matveich coolly. 'The economic principle is paramount.'

'My friend,' I cried, 'I'm going straight to the authorities to lodge a complaint. I can see we'll never sort out this mess on our own.'

'I agree with you,' said Ivan Matveich; 'however, during our present mercantile crisis it will be hard to lay open a crocodile's belly, gratis and without some

form of financial compensation; and then the unavoid-
able question arises—what will the proprietor accept
for his crocodile? And that raises a further question:
who is going to pay? For as you know, I have no
resources . . .'

'Perhaps an advance on your salary . . .' I remarked
cautiously; but the proprietor instantly broke in:

'I not sell crocodile! I sell crocodile three thousand,
I sell crocodile four thousand! Now *Publikum* shall very
much coming. I sell crocodile five thousand!'

In short, he was preening himself insufferably. His
whole face was aglow with repellent avarice and greed.

'I'm off!' I cried indignantly.

'I'm coming too! Me too! I'll go and see Andrei
Osipich himself, and melt him with my tears!' whim-
pered Elena Ivanovna.

'Don't do that, my dear,' Ivan Matveich hastily
interrupted her. He had long been jealous of his
wife's friendship with Andrei Osipich, and knew
that she would love to go and shed some tears before
that cultured individual, because tears were very
becoming to her. 'And I wouldn't advise you to do it
either, my friend,' he went on, addressing me; 'it's
pointless to rush at things in that hare-brained way;
there's no knowing what it could lead to. You'd do
much better to drop in on Timofei Semyonich, this

very day, just by way of a personal visit. He's old-fashioned and a bit stupid, but very respectable, and most importantly, he's a straight talker. Give him my compliments and describe what's happened. I owe him seven roubles from our last card game—it'll be the perfect opportunity to pay him, and that'll soften the stern old man. At all events, his advice could give us some useful guidance. But meanwhile, please take Elena Ivanovna away from here ... Don't fret, my dear,' he said to her, 'all these screams and women's brawls have worn me out, and I'd like a little nap now. It's warm and soft in here, though I haven't had time to look around my unexpected hiding place yet.'

'Look around! You mean it's light in there?' cried Elena Ivanovna in tones of relief.

'I'm plunged in impenetrable darkness,' replied the wretched prisoner, 'but I can feel my way round, and as it were, look about me with my hands ... Goodbye then, keep calm, and don't deny yourself any amusements. Until tomorrow! And you, Semyon Semyonich, come and see me tonight. Only, absent-minded as you are, you might easily forget, so tie a knot in your handkerchief ...'

I must confess that I was glad enough to get out of there myself—I was very tired, and also a bit bored. I quickly took Elena Ivanovna's arm; she was rather miserable, but her agitation had made her even prettier. I escorted her quickly out of the crocodile room.

'This evening again one quarter-rouble for entrance!' the proprietor called after us.

'My God, how greedy they are!' said Elena Ivanovna, checking her reflection in every mirror we passed in the Arcade, and obviously aware that she was looking her best.

'The economic principle,' I explained, feeling mildly excited and proud that the passers-by would notice the lady on my arm.

'The economic principle,' she said slowly, in a touching little voice. 'I didn't understand a word of what Ivan Matveich was saying just now, about that horrid economic principle.'

'Let me explain,' I answered, and immediately started telling her about the beneficial effects of attracting foreign capital to our own country, for I had been reading about them that very morning in *The Petersburg News* and *The Shout*.

'How strange this all is!' she interrupted me after listening for a while. 'Do stop, you horrid man, you're talking such nonsense . . . Tell me, is my face looking frightful?'

'Not frightful but delightful!' I told her, taking the opportunity to pay her a compliment.

'Naughty man!' she said complacently. 'Poor Ivan Matveich,' she added after a bit, tilting her head coquettishly. 'I'm sorry for him, I really am. Oh my God!' she cried suddenly, 'how on earth is he going to eat down there today? And . . . and . . . how is he going to . . . if he needs anything? . .'

'We hadn't thought of that,' I answered, nonplussed. To tell you the truth, the problem had never occurred to me. How much more practical women are than we menfolk, when it comes to the ordinary questions of everyday life!

'Poor darling, how could he have got into such a scrape . . . and nothing to amuse him, and so dark . . . and how upsetting that I haven't even got a photograph of him . . . So I'm a sort of widow now,' she added with a seductive smile, evidently intrigued by her new situation. 'Hmm! . . But I'm really sorry for him, all the same! . .'

It was, in short, the perfectly understandable and natural grief of a young and interesting wife for the husband she had lost. Eventually I saw her home, consoled her, dined with her, and after a cup of fragrant coffee I set off at six o'clock to find Timofei Semyonich, calculating that at that hour all family men of settled habits would be sitting—or lying down—at home.

Having related this first chapter in a style appropriate to the event I have described, I now propose to continue my account using less elevated but more natural language. The reader is warned.

II

The respected Timofei Semyonich greeted me hastily and rather nervously, ushering me into his cramped study and shutting the door firmly, 'so the children don't disturb us', he added, visibly anxious. He sat me down on his desk chair, seated himself in an armchair, wrapped his old wadded dressing gown tightly round him, and for safety's sake adopted an official air, looking almost stern in fact, although he was neither my chief nor Ivan Matveich's, and I had previously regarded him simply as a colleague and even a friend.

'First of all,' he began, 'remember I'm not someone in authority, I'm merely a subordinate official just like you and Ivan Matveich . . . This business is nothing to do with me, and I don't mean to get mixed up in anything.'

I was surprised to see that he seemed to know all about it already. Nevertheless I told him the whole story over again, in detail. I was talking in some agitation, for at that moment I was doing the duty of a true friend. He listened with no particular surprise, but with evident suspicion.

'Just imagine!' he said at the end of my account. 'I had always expected this very thing to happen to him.'

'Why was that, Timofei Semyonich? It's a most unusual thing to happen . . .'

'Agreed. But throughout his employment, Ivan Matveich has always been moving in that direction. Cocksure, in fact self-important. Always on about "progress" and all kinds of other ideas; but look where "progress" gets you!'

'But this was a most unusual event; you can't possibly mean it could happen to anyone who believes in progress!'

'Oh yes I can. You see, all this comes from too much education, believe me. Overeducated people are always sticking their noses into unsuitable things, instead of minding their own business. But perhaps you know better than me,' he added huffily. 'I'm an old man, and not particularly well educated. I started life as a soldier's son, and this year I celebrated my jubilee—fifty years in the service.'

'Not at all, Timofei Semyonich, please don't think that. On the contrary, Ivan Matveich is anxious for your advice, eager for your guidance. With tears in his eyes, as you might say.'

'Tears in his eyes, as you might say, eh? Hmm. Well, they're crocodile tears then, and not to be trusted. But what on earth tempted him to go abroad, tell me? And how was he going to pay for it? He doesn't have private means, does he?'

'He had saved up, Timofei Semyonich—from his last bonus,' I answered plaintively. 'And he only wanted to go for three months. To Switzerland . . . the land of William Tell.'

'William Tell, eh? Hmm!'

'And he wanted to see Naples in the springtime. And visit the museum, see how people live, see the animals . . .'

'Hmm! The animals, eh? I think it was nothing but vanity on his part. Animals? What animals? Don't we have enough animals here? We've got menageries, museums, camels . . . There are bears living right next to Petersburg. And he himself has ended up inside a crocodile . . .'

'Timofei Semyonich, I beg you, here's a man in desperate trouble, he's appealing to you as a friend, as an older relative; he's anxious for your advice, and you're just criticizing him . . . At least have pity on the wretched Elena Ivanovna!'

'You mean his wife? An interesting little lady,' said Timofei Semyonich, obviously relenting and taking a pinch of snuff with great relish. 'A fascinating creature. And so plump, and always tilting her head like that . . . tilting her head . . . very nice too. Andrei Osipich was talking about her a couple of days ago.'

'Talking about her?'

'Yes indeed, and in very flattering terms too. Such a bosom, he said, and such eyes, and such hair . . . A real sugarplum, he says, not a lady; and he laughed. He's a young man, of course,'—Timofei Semyonich blew his nose loudly—'yes, a young man, but what a career he's making for himself!'

'But this is something else entirely, Timofei Semyonich!'

'Yes, of course, of course.'

'So what do you think, Timofei Semyonich?'

'But what on earth can I do?'

'Give him some advice, give him some guidance, as a man of experience, as a relation! What steps can we take? Should we go to the authorities, or—'

'The authorities? Certainly not!' Timofei Semyonich replied hastily. 'If you want my advice, you should start by hushing the whole thing up, and only act as a private individual, as it were. It's a suspicious situation, completely unheard-of. Yes, unheard-of, that's important: this sort of thing has never happened before, and it doesn't look good . . . So it's vital to keep it quiet . . . Let him lie there for a bit. We must wait and see, wait and see . . .'

'How can we wait and see, Timofei Semyonich? What if he suffocates in there?'

'Why should he? I thought you said he had made himself reasonably comfortable?'

I told him the whole story again. Timofei Semyonich became thoughtful.

'Hmm!' he said, twisting his snuffbox in his fingers. 'I think it's actually a good idea for him to spend some time lying inside there, instead of travelling abroad. Leave him to think things out at leisure. Of course he mustn't suffocate, so proper steps will have to be taken to keep him in good health: well, avoid catching a cough, for instance, and so on . . . As for the German, my personal opinion is that he's in the right, even more so than the opposing party, because another person got into *his* crocodile without permission, it wasn't *he* who got into Ivan Matveich's crocodile without permission—in fact, so far as I can remember, Ivan Matveich has never even possessed a crocodile of his own. Well, and a crocodile constitutes an item of private property, so it may not be slit open without paying compensation.'

'But to save a human life, Timofei Semyonich!'

'Well, that's a police matter. You'll have to apply to them.'

'But Ivan Matveich might be needed in our department. He could be sent for.'

'Ivan Matveich—needed? Ha-ha! Besides, he's officially on leave now, so we can ignore him—let him look round the countries of Europe. Now if he doesn't turn up when his leave expires, that's a different matter. Then we'll ask around, make enquiries . . .'

'But—three months! Have a heart, Timofei Semyonich!'

'It's his own fault. Who shoved him in there? At this rate we'd have to hire an official nurse to look after him, and that's against regulations. But the main thing is—the crocodile is a property, so what they call the economic principle comes into play. And the economic principle is paramount. Only the other evening, at Luka Andreich's, Ignaty Prokofyich was talking—you know Ignaty Prokofyich? A capitalist, a big business-man and an excellent speaker. And he was saying, "What we need is industry; we have too little industry here. We need to create it. Therefore we need to create capital, we need to create a middle class, what they call a bourgeoisie. And since we don't have capital here, we have to attract it from abroad. First and foremost, we have to give foreign companies the opportunity to buy up Russian land, lot by lot, as they do everywhere abroad." Communal ownership of land is poison, he said, it's a disaster!—And you know, he was talking so heatedly—well, he can afford to, he's a very wealthy man, and not in the service . . . Under the communal system, he said, neither industry nor agriculture can flourish. What we need, he said, is for foreign companies to buy up the whole of our country, parcel by parcel, and then split it up, split it up as far as it will go, into small lots . . . and he said it so categorically, you know, *sssplit* it up, *sssplit* it up—and then sell it off as private property. No, not sell it off, just rent it out. And when every bit of land is in the hands of the foreign companies we've attracted over here, then they can set any rent they like. So the peasant will work three times harder than before, just to earn his daily bread, and he can be turned out at will. He'll be aware of that, and he'll be docile, and industrious, and work three times as hard for the same money. Whereas now, under the commune, what does he care? He knows he won't die of starvation, so he grows lazy and drunken. At the same time money will come into the country, and there'll be capital, and a bourgeoisie will grow up.

Recently *The Times*, the English political and literary paper, had an article about our finances; it said that the reason we don't have financial growth is that we don't have a middle class, nor any big fortunes, nor a willing working class ... He talks well, does Ignaty Prokofyich. A real orator. He wants to present a paper to the authorities and then have it published in *The Petersburg News*. That's a long way from Ivan Matveich and his hot air.'

'So what about Ivan Matveich, then?' I put in, after letting the old man get all that off his chest. Timofei Semyonich liked to let off steam every so often, just to prove that he wasn't behind the times, but knew what was what.

'Ivan Matveich? But that's what I was talking about. Here we are, doing our best to attract foreign capital to Russia, and then—judge for yourself. We've attracted a crocodile owner to this country, with his capital which, thanks to Ivan Matveich, has now doubled, and yet, instead of protecting a foreign property owner, we're doing our best to take his basic capital and slit its belly open. What's the sense of that? To my mind, Ivan Matveich, as a true son of his fatherland, should be rejoicing and feeling proud of the fact that by his very person he has doubled, if not tripled, the value of a foreign crocodile. That's what needs to be done to attract more capital. Where one person has succeeded, you can be sure that another will arrive with his own crocodile, and then a third, with two or three crocodiles at once, and their capital will grow and grow. That's the bourgeoisie for you. It has to be encouraged.'

'For pity's sake, Timofei Semyonich!' I cried, 'You're demanding almost superhuman self-sacrifice from poor Ivan Matveich!'

'I'm not demanding anything; and above all I must remind you once more to bear in mind that I am not a person in authority, and consequently in no position to demand anything from anyone. I was speaking as a son of the fatherland—I mean, not as "The Son of the Fatherland", but merely as a son of our fatherland. But I ask you again, who ever ordered him to climb into a crocodile? Here's a respectable man, of a certain rank, lawfully married, and suddenly—to take such a step! How does that make sense?'

'But that step happened accidentally.'

'Who knows? And then, where is the money to come from, to pay the crocodile keeper, eh? Tell me that!'

'Perhaps an advance on his salary, Timofei Semyonich?'

'Will there be enough?'

'No, there won't, Timofei Semyonich,' I answered sadly. 'The crocodile keeper was scared at first that his crocodile would burst, but then, when he could see that all was well, he started preening himself with delight at the prospect of doubling the entrance fee.'

'Or even tripling or quadrupling it! The public will stampede the place now—and these crocodile keepers are canny people. Besides which, it's not Lent yet, people are on the lookout for amusements—so I repeat, the most important thing is for Ivan Matveich to stay incognito and not be in any hurry. Actually, everyone can know that he's in the crocodile, but without knowing it officially. From that point of view, Ivan Matveich is in a particularly fortunate position, because he's officially abroad. People will say that he's in the crocodile, and we won't believe them. That's how it could be managed. The main thing is to stay put, and wait. What's the hurry, anyway?'

'Well, but supposing . . .'

'Don't worry, he has a sound constitution.'

'But later on, after he's waited?'

'Well, I can't pretend that it isn't a most exceptional case. No idea what to make of it. The worst of it is that there's never been anything like it before. If we had a precedent, now, we might have something to go by. But as it is, what can one say? It could drag on a very long time before it's sorted out.'

A happy thought flashed through my mind.

'Couldn't we arrange things,' I suggested, 'so that if he's doomed to remain in the monster's entrails, and if Providence decrees that he remain alive—couldn't he submit a petition to have himself classed as still serving?'

'Hmm . . . perhaps on unpaid leave . . .'

'No, couldn't he keep his salary?'

'On what basis?'

'Sent on some special mission . . .'

'What sort of mission? Where?'

'To the crocodile's innards, I mean . . . Gathering information, as it were; studying the situation on the ground. That would be a new departure, of course, but it would be forward-looking, and demonstrate educational zeal . . .'

Timofei Semyonich thought a bit.

'Sending a dedicated official on a mission to a crocodile's innards,' he finally said, 'to conduct a special inquiry—in my personal opinion that's absurd. It's not in the regulations. And what could he be instructed to do in there?'

'Oh, to make a scientific study of nature in its normal habitat, *in vivo*, as it were. The natural sciences are all the rage these days, you know—botany, and all that . . . He could be living there and reporting back . . . on, say, the creature's digestion, or even just its habits, you know. Fact-finding.'

'You mean, a statistical study. Well, that's not my forte. And I'm not a philosopher. You talk of facts—but we're deluged with facts as it is, and we don't know what to do with them. Besides, statistics are risky.'

'In what way?'

'They're risky. And moreover, don't forget—he'll be reporting facts while he's lying on his side. But can you report facts while lying on your side? That would be a further novelty, and a dangerous one; and once again, there's no precedent for it. Now if we had just the tiniest little precedent, then in my view we might have sent him on a mission like that.'

'But no one has ever imported a live crocodile before, Timofei Semyonich.'

'Hmm, yes . . .' He paused for thought again. 'Well, I grant you, your objection is a fair one, in fact it might even serve as the basis for taking the matter further. But again, you have to bear this in mind: if live crocodiles start arriving here and then employees start to disappear, and it's so warm and cosy down there that people demand to be sent on missions in there, and then they just lie around . . . you must admit, that sets a bad example. Everybody would start getting into crocodiles, to earn money for doing nothing.'

'Do what you can, Timofei Semyonich! Incidentally, Ivan Matveich asked me to pay you a little debt, seven roubles he lost to you at cards.'

'Ah yes, he lost that the other day, at Nikifor Nikiforovich's! I remember. And how jolly he was that night, made us all laugh—and now, look! . .'

The old man was genuinely moved.

'Do what you can, Timofei Semyonich.'

'I'll do my best. I'll raise it in my own name, as a private matter, a request for information. Actually, could you find out, just unofficially, as a third party— how much would the keeper accept for his crocodile?'

Timofei Semyonich had become visibly more friendly.

'Certainly,' I replied, 'and I'll come straight back to you with his answer.'

'What about his wife . . . all on her own now? Missing him?'

'You ought to drop in on her, Timofei Semyonich.'

'And so I shall; I'd been thinking about it earlier. And this is a good opportunity. But what on earth, what on earth came over him, to go and look at a crocodile!—Actually, I wouldn't mind taking a look myself.'

'Go and visit the poor man, Timofei Semyonich.'

'I shall. But of course I don't want to raise his hopes by taking that step. I'll go as a private individual. Well, goodbye—I'm on my way to Nikifor Nikiforovich's again; will you be there?'

'No, I'm off to visit the prisoner.'

'There you are, you see—the prisoner! Oh my, how thoughtless of him!'

I took my leave of the old man. My head was buzzing with all kinds of thoughts. Such a kind, honourable person, our Timofei Semyonich; and yet as I left him, I felt pleased that he'd already celebrated his fiftieth anniversary in his post, and that people like him are a rarity these days. Needless to say, I rushed back to the Arcade to tell poor Ivan Matveich all about my visit. I was tormented by curiosity, too: how was he getting on inside the crocodile—and how could a person live inside a crocodile at all? Indeed, was it at all possible to live in a crocodile? Sometimes the whole thing seemed to me no more than a monstrous dream—particularly as it was all about a monster . . .

III

And yet it was no dream, but actual, undoubted fact. Would I ever have started telling this tale otherwise? But let me continue . . .

I reached the Arcade late, about nine o'clock, and had to get to the crocodile room by the back entrance, since the German had locked up earlier than usual. He was strolling about with an air of complacent domesticity, wearing a scruffy, greasy old frock coat, evidently three times more pleased with himself even than that morning. I could see that nothing worried him now, and that '*Publikum* much coming'. The Mutter only came out later, evidently to keep an eye on me. The two of them kept exchanging whispers. Although the booth was closed, he still charged me my quarter-rouble. How pointlessly punctilious of him!

'You every time shall paying. *Publikum* pay one rouble, but you only quarter, because you good friend of your good friend, and I honour friend!'

'Is he alive? Is he alive, my cultured friend?' I called loudly as I approached the crocodile, hoping that my words might reach Ivan Matveich from a distance and flatter his vanity.

'Alive and well,' he called back, sounding far away or as if he was under a bed—though by now I was standing beside him. 'Alive and well, but we'll come back to that. How did it go?'

I purposely pretended not to hear his question, and began asking him with sympathetic urgency how he was, what was happening to him, how he felt inside the crocodile, and what a crocodile's inside was like . . . I owed him that out of friendship and common politeness. But he interrupted me capriciously and irritably.

'How did it go?' he shouted, bossily as ever, in his shrill voice, which just then I found particularly repellent.

I told him all about my talk with Timofei Semyonich, down to the last detail, trying to keep an injured note in my voice as I spoke.

'The old man's right,' decided Ivan Matveich, speaking just as curtly as he always did to me. 'I like practical people. I can't stand sentimental softies. But I grant that your idea of an official mission isn't entirely ridiculous. There really is a lot of information I could give, both from a scientific and moral point of view. But everything has now taken a new and unexpected turn. There's no point fussing about my salary alone. Listen carefully. Are you sitting down?'

'No, I'm standing.'

'Sit down on something—on the floor, if need be. And listen carefully.'

Furiously I grabbed a chair, banging it down on the floor in my annoyance.

'Listen,' he began imperiously, 'there was a huge crowd of people here today. By evening there was no room, and the police had to come and keep order. At eight o'clock, earlier than the normal closing time, the owner had to shut up shop and close the exhibition so as to count up the entrance money and make proper preparations for tomorrow. And I know that tomorrow the place will be a regular fairground. So we have to assume that all the most cultured inhabitants of this capital city, high society ladies, foreign envoys, lawyers and so forth, will be turning up. And that's not all. People will arrive from all the multitudinous provinces of our far-flung and fascinating empire. And consequently I shall be on show to everyone—concealed, but the centre of interest nonetheless. And I'll instruct this idle crowd. Taught by experience, I shall become an example of greatness of spirit and resignation to my fate! I shall be, as you might say, a podium from which I shall set myself to educate mankind. Even the mere scientific details that I can provide about the monster I now inhabit will be of immense value. For which reason, I no longer rail against my present fate, but hold out confident hopes of a most brilliant career.'

'Won't you be bored?' I asked spitefully.

What annoyed me most of all was his pompous language and self-importance. But at the same time I couldn't make head or tail of his attitude. 'What on earth is making this airhead so cocksure?' I whispered to myself through gritted teeth. 'He ought to be weeping, not bragging.'

'No!' he answered me sharply. 'Imbued as I am with exalted ideas, it is only now that I can meditate at leisure about improving the destiny of all mankind. Out of a crocodile, truth and light shall emerge. I shall most certainly formulate a personal theory of modern economic relations, and I shall take pride in it—which I have hitherto been unable to do, due to the demands of my official duties and the trivial distractions of daily life. I shall refute everything and become the new Fourier. Incidentally, did you pay Timofei Semyonich those seven roubles?'

'Out of my own pocket,' I said, trying to make my voice reflect the fact.

'We'll settle up,' he replied in a lordly voice. 'I'm expecting an increase in my salary imminently— after all, who deserves a rise better than me? I'm a man of infinite value now. But back to business. My wife?'

'I expect you're asking about Elena Ivanovna?'

'My wife!' he fairly shrieked.

There was no help for it! Meekly, but again grinding my teeth, I told him how I had left Elena Ivanovna. He didn't even hear me out.

'I have special plans for her,' he interrupted impatiently. 'If I am going to be famous *here*, I want her to be famous *there*. Scholars, poets, philosophers, visiting mineralogists, statesmen—after a morning's conversation with me, they will visit her salon in the evenings. From next week, she must hold an evening salon every day. With my salary doubled, we can pay for the receptions, and as there will only be tea, and the footmen will be hired, the whole thing is settled. People will be talking about me both here and there. It has been a long-established ambition of mine to have everyone talking about me, but I could not bring it about because I was not important and high-ranking enough. And now it's all been achieved, thanks to nothing more than the gulp of a crocodile. Every word I utter will be listened to, every pronouncement I make will be weighed up, and passed on, and printed. And I'll make sure I'm known! People will eventually realize what talents they have allowed to vanish into a crocodile's innards. "This man might have been foreign minister, he could have ruled a kingdom," they'll say. "But alas, this man never did rule a foreign kingdom," others will say. But how, in what way, am I inferior to some Garnier-Pagèsichky or whatever he's called? And my wife must be my opposite number—I have the brains, she has the beauty and charm. "She's beautiful, that's why she's his wife," some will say. "She's beautiful, *because* she's his wife," others will put them right. Tomorrow, to be on the safe side, Elena

Ivanovna must buy Andrei Kraevsky's *Encyclopaedic Dictionary*, so that she can talk on any subject. But her most regular reading must be "Premier-Politic" in *The Petersburg News*, which she must compare daily with *The Shout*. I suppose that the crocodile owner will agree to bring me along from time to time, together with the crocodile, to my wife's brilliant salon. My tank, with me inside, will stand in the middle of the splendid reception room and I will pour out a stream of witticisms, which I shall have prepared that morning. To the statesman, I shall describe my projects; to the poet, I shall talk in rhyme; with the ladies I shall be amusing and charming without immodesty—since I present no danger whatsoever to their husbands. To everyone else, I shall serve as a model of submission to destiny and the will of Providence. I shall raise up my wife to become a brilliant lady of letters, I shall make her known, I shall explain to her admirers that as my wife, she must be endowed with all the most striking virtues. If Andrei Alexandrovich is rightly known as the Russian Alfred de Musset, it will be only fair for her to be called our Russian Evgenia Tur.'

I must confess that although all this wild raving was fairly typical of Ivan Matveich, it did nevertheless occur to me that he might have become feverish and delirious. This was the same ordinary, everyday Ivan

Matveich, but observed through a lens that magnified him twenty times.

'My friend, are you looking forward to a long life?' I asked. 'Tell me, are you well? How do you eat, how do you sleep, how do you breathe? I'm your friend, and you must allow that your case is so excessively supernatural that my curiosity is excessively natural.'

'Idle curiosity, and nothing more,' he replied pompously; 'but you shall be satisfied. You ask how I am getting along in the monster's entrails? First of all, the crocodile, to my surprise, turned out to be quite empty. His insides consist of something like an enormous empty bag made of rubber, like those elastic items that are available here on Gorokhovaya or Morskaya Streets, or—if I'm not mistaken—on Voznesensky Prospect. Otherwise how do you imagine I could fit inside?'

'Can that be so?' I exclaimed in very natural astonishment. 'Is the crocodile really completely empty?'

'Completely,' pronounced Ivan Matveich sternly and impressively. 'And in all probability, it is made that way according to the laws of Nature herself. The crocodile possesses only jaws equipped with sharp teeth, and in addition to its jaws, an extremely long tail. That is really all there is to it. In the middle, between those two extremities, there is an empty space enclosed in something resembling rubber—most probably, indeed, it actually is rubber.'

'But the ribs, the stomach, the intestines, the liver, the heart?' I interrupted him furiously.

'N-no, nothing whatever of that sort, and probably there never was. That is all an idle fantasy of empty-headed travellers. Just as people inflate a rubber ring cushion, so I am now inflating the crocodile by my presence. It is distensible to an incredible degree. Even you, as a family friend, could fit in here beside me, if you were generous-hearted enough—and even with you here, there would still be room. I am even considering, if it comes to it, sending for Elena Ivanovna. Anyway, this totally empty body construction is entirely consistent with natural science. Just imagine you were tasked with designing a new crocodile. You would immediately ask yourself: what is the fundamental crocodilian characteristic? Answer: swallowing people, of course. How to design a crocodile to enable it to swallow people? Answer, even more obviously: make it empty. Physical science long ago determined that nature abhors a vacuum. Consequently the crocodilian interior must also be empty, so that, abhorring a vacuum, it is forced incessantly to swallow and replenish itself with whatever is at hand. And this is the sole logical reason why all crocodiles swallow our fellow men. The same is not true of the human organism: the emptier a human head is, for example, the less it feels the urge to fill itself; this is the only exception to the general rule. All this is now as clear as day to me; I have worked it out from my own experience and intellect, situated as I am, so to speak, in the very bowels of nature, in its very crucible, hearkening to the beating of its pulse. Etymology, too, is on my side: the crocodile's very name indicates voracity. Crocodile, *crocodillo*—it must be an Italian word, perhaps dating back to the days of the ancient Egyptian pharaohs, and clearly derived from the French root *croquer*, meaning to eat, to devour, to ingest as food. I intend to expound all this in my first lecture to my public when they assemble in Elena Ivanovna's salon, and I am conveyed there in my tank.'

'My friend, shouldn't you at least take a laxative?' I couldn't help crying out. 'He's feverish, feverish, he's in a fever!' I repeated to myself in horror.

'Nonsense!' he retorted contemptuously. 'Besides, in my present position that would be quite inconvenient. As a matter of fact, I more or less knew that you would raise the question of a laxative.'

'But my friend, how . . . how do you take food now? Have you dined today, or not?'

'No, but I am full, and most probably I shall never take food again. And this, too, is entirely understandable: since I myself fill the whole interior of this crocodile, I cause the creature to feel permanently full. Now it may do without feeding for several years. And conversely, being full of me, it will naturally share with me all the vital juices of its body; it will be like those refined coquettes, who cover their entire persons with raw steaks before retiring, and then, after their morning bath, become fresh, supple, juicy and seductive. So it is that I, in feeding the crocodile upon myself, receive nourishment from it in return; we mutually nourish one another. But it is difficult, even for the crocodile, to digest such a person as myself; for in the process it must naturally experience some heaviness in its stomach—which, by the way, it does not possess; and this is why, in order not to cause the monster unnecessary pain, I rarely turn over from side to side. Although I would be physically able to turn over, I avoid doing so for humanitarian reasons. This is the only drawback of my present situation, and in an allegorical sense Timofei Semyonich is correct when he calls me a layabout. But I shall prove that even when lying on my side—nay indeed, *only* when lying on my side—I can turn around the destiny of mankind. All the great ideas and movements promoted by our newspapers and magazines have evidently been created by layabouts; that's why their ideas are dismissed as armchair thinking—but who cares what they're called! I am now about to invent a whole new social system—you can't believe how easy that is. All you need is to get away on your own somewhere, far from other people, in a corner, or inside a crocodile, say, and shut your eyes, and in a moment you've invented a whole paradise for all mankind. Earlier on, when you all left, I got down to inventing; I've already invented three systems, and now I'm working on a fourth. True, you have to start by refuting everything; but it's so easy to refute it all from inside a crocodile. In a crocodile, everything actually seems so much clearer . . . As a matter of fact, there are some other drawbacks in my situation, but they're trivial ones. It's rather damp in here, and everything seems to be coated with slime; and then it rather smells of rubber, like last year's old galoshes. That's all, there aren't any other drawbacks.'

'Ivan Matveich,' I interrupted him, 'I can hardly believe in this string of miracles. And are you really, really, never in your life going to eat dinner again?'

'What a fuss you're making about trivial rubbish, you idle, empty-headed man! I'm talking to you about great ideas, while you . . . You must understand that I am filled to repletion with these great ideas, which have illuminated the dark night that surrounds me. Though as a matter of fact, the good-natured keeper of this monster, after discussion with that most kind-hearted Mutter, has agreed to pass a bent metal tube between the crocodile's jaws every morning, something like a musical pipe, through which I shall be able to suck coffee, or broth with white bread soaked in it. The pipe has already been ordered from a local supplier, though in my view it is an unnecessary luxury. And I expect to live for at least a thousand years, if that is indeed a crocodile's lifespan—which reminds me, look it up in a natural history book tomorrow and let me know, for I may have made a mistake and confused the crocodile with some other excavated monster. There is only one consideration that somewhat troubles me: since I am dressed in cloth, with boots on my feet, the crocodile will evidently not be able to digest me. Furthermore, I am alive, and therefore resist being digested with all my willpower, since understandably I do not wish to be converted into that which is the end product of any other form of food; that would be too degrading. But there is one thing I am afraid of: over the course of a thousand years, the cloth of my frock coat, regrettably of Russian manufacture, may perish; and then, remaining without clothing, I may—for all my indignation— begin to be digested. And although by day I shall certainly not allow this to happen, once I am asleep at night, when a man's will deserts him, I may be subjected to the same most humiliating fate as any potato, pancake or veal cutlet. The very idea infuriates me. That consideration alone should be sufficient for this country to alter its tariffs and encourage the import of English fabrics, which are tougher and consequently would hold out for longer against the effects of nature, should one happen to find oneself in a crocodile. I shall take the first opportunity to communicate my idea to some statesman, and to the political columnists on our Petersburg daily papers. Let them proclaim it abroad. I hope that this will not be the only idea of mine that they adopt. I foresee a whole crowd of them, each armed with his quarter-rouble from the newspaper office, thronging around me every morning to pick up my thoughts on the previous day's telegrams. In short, I see my future in the rosiest light.'

'Feverish, feverish!' I whispered to myself.

'But my friend, what about freedom?' I asked, wishing to discover exactly what he thought. 'After all, you're in a prison cell, as it were, whereas a human being ought to be enjoying his freedom.'

'You're a fool,' he replied. 'Savages love independence, but wise men love order. And where there is no order . . .'

'Ivan Matveich, I beg you! . .'

'Silence, and listen to me!' he yelled, furious at being interrupted. 'Never has my spirit soared aloft as it does now. In my narrow refuge, I fear only one thing: the literary criticisms of our fat journals and the hisses of our satirical papers. I fear being mocked by empty-headed visitors, envious fools and nihilists in general. But I shall take all necessary steps. I impatiently await the public's reactions tomorrow morning, and most particularly the opinions of the newspapers. Let me know about the newspapers as soon as they appear.'

'Very well, I shall bring you a whole pile of newspapers, tomorrow as ever is.'

'Tomorrow is too soon to expect reactions in the newspapers, for announcements are only printed on the fourth day. But from now on, come here each evening, through the inner entry from the courtyard. I intend to use you as my secretary. You shall read me the newspapers and journals, and I shall dictate my thoughts to you and commission you to run my errands. In particular, do not forget the telegrams. All the European telegrams must be brought to me every day. But that will do for now—you probably want to get some sleep. Be off home, and forget what I've just said about criticism: I do not fear it, for criticism is itself in crisis. All that is needed is to be wise and virtuous, and one is sure to be raised on a pedestal. If not as a Socrates, then as a Diogenes, or the two together; and such is my future role among humankind.'

Ivan Matveich was rattling on unthinkingly and obsessively (true, he was in a fever), like one of those weak-willed women who, the proverb tells us, can never keep a secret. Everything he told me about the crocodile seemed highly suspicious to me. How could it possibly be true that the animal was completely empty? I'd have taken a bet that he was just boasting, perhaps out of vanity, perhaps partly to humiliate me. Of course he was sick, and a sick man has to be humoured; but I must admit in all honesty that I had always detested Ivan Matveich. All my life, from childhood on, I had longed in vain to escape from his officious care. A thousand times over, I wanted to break with him altogether, but each time I was drawn back, as though still hoping to prove something to him and somehow get my revenge on him. What an odd friendship it was! I can positively affirm that nine-tenths of it was founded on fury. However, on this occasion we said goodbye with genuine feeling.

'Your friend is very clever man,' murmured the German as he was about to see me out. He had been listening keenly to our whole conversation.

'*À propos,*' I said, 'while I think of it—how much would you accept for your crocodile, if someone wanted to buy it from you?'

Ivan Matveich heard my question, and awaited the answer with interest. It was obvious that he did not want the German to accept a low price; at all events, he cleared his throat in a meaningful way when I asked.

At first the German would not even hear me, and became quite angry.

'Nobody dare my own crocodile to buy!' he yelled, turning as red as a boiled lobster. 'I not want crocodile to sell. I will not one million thalers take for crocodile. I take today from *Publikum* one hundred thirty thalers, tomorrow I take ten thousand thalers, afterwards every day one hundred thousand thalers. I want not him to sell!'

Ivan Matveich fairly chortled with delight.

Forcing myself to talk coolly and soberly—for I was doing the duty of a true friend—I reminded this hot-headed German that his calculations were not quite accurate. That if he were to take a hundred thousand a day, then by the end of four days the whole of Petersburg would have visited, and after that he would take no money at all. Also that life and death were in God's hands, and the crocodile might burst, or Ivan Matveich might fall ill and die, et cetera, et cetera.

The German became thoughtful. 'I will giving him drops from pharmacy,' he finally said, 'and your friend not die.'

'Drops are all very well,' said I, 'but remember that you may find yourself involved with the law. Ivan Matveich's wife can demand to have her lawful husband restored to her. You're determined to make your fortune, but do you intend to give Elena Ivanovna anything at all by way of a pension?'

'No! Not intend!' replied the German, sternly and decisively.

'No! Not intend!' Mutter repeated, quite spitefully.

'In which case, wouldn't you do better to accept something now, on the spot—a modest sum, but a secure and solid one, rather than leave everything to chance? I have to make it clear that I am not asking out of idle curiosity.'

The German took Mutter's arm and went off to consult with her, in the corner with the cage containing the biggest and ugliest of his whole collection of monkeys.

'Now you'll see!' said Ivan Matveich.

As far as I was concerned, at that point I was burning with the desire, firstly, to give the German a painful thrashing, secondly, to give Mutter an even more painful thrashing, but thirdly, to give the hardest and most painful thrashing of all to Ivan Matveich for his boundless vanity. Yet all this paled into insignificance compared with the avaricious German's eventual answer.

After consulting with Mutter, he demanded, as the price of his crocodile, fifty thousand roubles in bonds of the latest Russian loan with lottery vouchers attached, plus a stone mansion on Gorokhovaya Street with its own pharmacy; and on top of all that, the rank of a Russian colonel.

'See!' shouted Ivan Matveich triumphantly, 'what did I tell you! And apart from his final crazy desire to be promoted colonel, he's absolutely right, since he fully understands the current value of the monster he has on display. The economic principle is paramount!'

'For goodness' sake!' I shouted furiously at the German. 'Why on earth should you be made a colonel? What exploit have you performed, what service have you done, what military glory have you earned? You're stark staring mad!'

'Mad!' cried the injured German, 'No, I very clever person, and you very stupid! I have colonel deserved, because I crocodile show, with in him one live *Hofrat* sits, and Russian cannot crocodile show, with in him one live *Hofrat* sits! I one exceptional clever person and very much want colonel become!'

'Goodbye then, Ivan Matveich!' I shouted, quivering with rage, and almost ran out of the crocodile room. Another minute, I felt, and I could no longer have answered for my actions. The preposterous aspirations of these two blockheads were more than I could bear. Out in the fresh air, I cooled down and felt a little less indignant. At last I spat to both sides some fifteen times, took a cab home, undressed and flung myself into bed. The most annoying thing of all was that I had become his secretary. Now I would have to die of boredom there every evening, doing the duty of a true friend! I could have pummelled myself for that, and indeed, when I had blown out my candle and pulled up the bedclothes, I did punch myself a few times, on the head and other parts of my body. That made me feel a bit better, and eventually I fell asleep and slept quite soundly, because I was very tired. All night I dreamt of nothing but monkeys, but towards morning I did have a dream about Elena Ivanovna . . .

IV

The monkeys, I realized, had got into my dreams because they were locked in a cage at the crocodile keeper's; but Elena Ivanovna was a different matter.

Let me say straight away—I loved that lady. But I hasten—post-haste—to explain: I loved her as a father, neither more nor less. I conclude that this was so, because I often felt an overpowering longing to kiss her, on her little head or her rosy cheek. And although I had never carried out this desire, I confess ... I would not have turned down the chance of kissing her on her lips either. And not only her lips, but her little teeth, which peeped out so sweetly, like two rows of pretty, well-matched pearls, whenever she laughed. She laughed amazingly often. In moments of tenderness, Ivan Matveich used to call her his 'darling bit of nonsense'—which was absolutely right and appropriate. She was a delicious titbit, that was all there was to it. So I simply have no idea why that same Ivan Matveich suddenly saw her as a Russian Evgenia Tur. Anyway, my dream—leaving aside the monkeys—had left me with the pleasantest of feelings. As I reflected on the previous day's events over my morning cup of tea, I decided to drop in on Elena Ivanovna straight away, on my way to work—which was my duty in any case, simply as a friend of the family.

In a tiny room next to her bedroom, in what they called their little drawing room (though their big drawing room was also small), on a smart little sofa by a little tea table, sat Elena Ivanovna, wearing a sort of flimsy morning gown and sipping coffee out of a little cup into which she was dipping a tiny biscuit. She was ravishingly beautiful, but at the same time struck me as rather thoughtful.

'Ah, it's you, you naughty boy!' she greeted me, with an absent smile. 'Sit down, madcap, and have some coffee. So what did you get up to yesterday? Did you come to the masked ball?'

'Why, were you there? I don't go out, you know . . . Besides, yesterday I was visiting our prisoner . . .'

I sighed, and put on a righteous expression as I was handed my coffee.

'Who? What prisoner? Oh yes, him! Poor lamb! Well, and how is he? Bored? You know what? . . I wanted to ask you . . . I can apply for a divorce now, can't I?'

'Divorce!' I cried out indignantly, almost spilling my coffee. 'It's that swarthy little fellow!' I thought in fury.

There was a certain swarthy individual with a little moustache, employed in the architectural section, who was far too fond of visiting them, and particularly good at making Elena Ivanovna laugh. I must confess I hated him, and there was no doubt that he had already managed to see Elena Ivanovna the evening before, either at the masked ball or even here in her own home, and fill her head with all kinds of nonsense.

'I mean to say,' Elena Ivanovna went on rapidly, as if someone had been coaching her, 'what if he stays stuck inside the crocodile, and never comes out again in his life—am I supposed just to wait for him? A husband should be living in his home, not in a crocodile.'

'But this was an unforeseen event,' I began, naturally feeling very agitated.

'No, no! Don't go on! I don't want to listen, I don't!' she cried, suddenly very angry. 'You're always against me, you horrid man! What use are you—you'll never give me any advice! Other people have told me I'd get a divorce, because Ivan Matveich won't be getting his salary any more.'

'Elena Ivanovna! Is this you talking?' I exclaimed pathetically. 'What villain could have put such ideas into your head? Anyway, divorce on such trivial grounds as a salary is quite impossible. But there's poor, poor Ivan Matveich, burning with love for you, so to speak, even down there in the monster's innards. He's simply melting away with love, like a sugar lump. Just yesterday evening, while you were enjoying yourself at the masked ball, he mentioned that as a last resort, he might perhaps decide to have you sent in to him as his lawful wife, down into the bowels of the monster—particularly as the crocodile turns out to be exceedingly spacious, with room for not even two, but three people . . .'

And then I told her all that interesting part of my yesterday's conversation with Ivan Matveich.

'What? What?' she cried out in astonishment. 'You want me to climb down there too, just to be with Ivan Matveich? The very idea! And how could I get down there, in my little hat and crinoline? Good God, what a stupid plan! And what sort of a figure will I cut, climbing in there, and somebody's sure to be looking at me while I do it . . . Ridiculous! And what'll I eat down there? . . and . . . and how will I manage, when . . . Oh my God, what on earth have they dreamt up! . . And how will I amuse myself down there? . . You say it smells of indiarubber? And what if we have a quarrel—are we still supposed to go on lying side by side? Ugh, what a revolting idea!'

'I agree, I agree with everything you say, my dearest Elena Ivanovna,' I interrupted, striving to express myself with that natural animation that always inspires a man when he feels he has right on his side. 'But you've forgotten one thing. You haven't appreciated the fact that he clearly can't live without you, if he's calling on you to join him; in other words, this is love—passionate, true, ardent love . . . You haven't appreciated his love, dear Elena Ivanovna; remember his love!'

'I won't, I won't, and I won't listen to another word!' she insisted, brushing my words aside with her pretty little hand, with its rosy nails newly washed and scrubbed. 'Horrible man! You're going to make me cry! Get in there yourself, if you like the idea. You're his friend, aren't you? Well then, lie down beside him like his best friend, and you can spend your lives arguing about boring science or something . . .'

'You're wrong to laugh at the idea like this,' I checked the empty-headed woman with great dignity. 'Ivan Matveich has invited me down there as it is. Of course, your duty calls you, while I am moved by generosity alone. But yesterday, when Ivan Matveich was telling me about the crocodile's remarkable elasticity, he hinted very plainly that not only the two of you, but I too, as a friend of the family, could fit in there beside you, all three of us together, particularly if it was something I wished to do; and so . . .'

'What, the three of us together?' cried Elena Ivanovna, staring at me in astonishment. 'But how could we . . . all three of us be there together? Ha-ha-ha! How stupid you both are! Ha-ha-ha! I'll keep on pinching you all the time in there, you wicked man! Ha-ha-ha! Ha-ha-ha!'

She flung herself back on the sofa and laughed till the tears came to her eyes. The whole thing—her tears, and her laughter—was so seductive that I couldn't control myself, but began passionately kissing her hands; she didn't try to stop me, but she tweaked my ears a bit as a sign of reconciliation.

After that we both got quite merry, and I told her all the details of Ivan Matveich's plans, which he had described to me the night before. The idea of holding receptions and hosting a salon greatly appealed to her.

'But I'll need a lot of new gowns,' she pointed out, 'so Ivan Matveich will have to send me all the money he can, as quick as he can . . . Only . . . only how . . .' she added doubtfully, 'how are they going to bring him to me in the crocodile tank? That's quite ridiculous. I don't want my husband to be carried around in a tank. It would be too embarrassing, in front of all the guests . . . I don't want that. No, I don't want it.'

'Incidentally, before I forget: did Timofei Semyonich come and see you last night?'

'Oh yes, he came to comfort me, and just imagine, we spent the whole evening playing cards. He played for sweets, and if I lost, he could kiss my hands. Such a rascal—and just imagine, he almost came along to the masked ball with me. Honestly!'

'He got carried away!' I remarked. 'But who wouldn't—you're such a seductive creature!'

'Oh, get along with you and your compliments! Wait a second, let me give you a pinch to send you on your way. I've got terribly good at pinching people these days. See, how about that! Yes, incidentally, you said that Ivan Matveich talked a lot about me last night?'

'N-n-no, not all that much ... I must admit, he mostly thinks about the destiny of mankind, and he wants—'

'Good luck to him! No, don't tell me all about it, it's probably deadly boring. I'll go round and see him one of these days. I'll go tomorrow, definitely. Only not today. I've got a headache, and besides, there'll be lots of people there ... They'll say—here's his wife; and I'll feel embarrassed. Goodbye. Tonight you'll be ... there?'

'Yes, I'll be with him, certainly. He told me to come, and bring the newspapers.'

'Well, that's fine. You go and visit him, and read to him. But don't come here tonight. I'm not well—and I may go out to see some people. Off you go, you madcap.'

'That dark-skinned fellow will be round this evening,' I thought to myself.

At the office, of course, I gave no sign of being so consumed by these cares and troubles. But that morning I soon noticed copies of some of our most progressive newspapers being briskly passed from hand to hand among my colleagues, and being perused with extremely serious expressions. The first to come my way was *The Leaflet*, a news-sheet with no particular political affiliation but a generally humanitarian outlook, so most of us despised it, though we still read it. It was with some surprise that I came across the following:

'Extraordinary rumours were spreading yesterday through our great capital city, rich in such splendid edifices. A certain N., a well-known gastronome from the upper echelons of society, weary no doubt of the cuisine of Borel and the —— Club, paid a visit to the Arcade and entered the booth where a gigantic crocodile was on display, having just been brought over to the capital. He demanded to have the crocodile prepared and cooked for his dinner. Having come to an agreement with the proprietor, he immediately set about consuming him (not the proprietor, that is—a highly peaceable and punctilious-minded German— but his crocodile), which he ate alive, carving off juicy morsels with his penknife and swallowing them with extraordinary rapidity. Bit by bit, the whole crocodile vanished into the man's capacious stomach, after which he was actually preparing to attack an ichneumon, the crocodile's constant companion, probably imagining that the latter would be no less delicious. We are by no means opposed to this new foodstuff, long familiar to foreign gastronomes. We had even foreseen such a fashion. English lords and travellers in Egypt join in regular crocodile-hunting parties, during which they carve the monster's back to provide beef-steaks which they consume with mustard, onions and potatoes. The French, who arrived with de Lesseps, opt for the feet baked in hot ashes, with the aim of provoking the English who laugh at them. Here in Russia, both recipes are likely to find favour. For our part, we welcome this new branch of the culinary art, sadly wanting in our mighty and richly varied fatherland. Now that this first crocodile has vanished into the stomach of a Petersburg gastronome, it is likely that not a year will pass before crocodiles are imported into Russia in their hundreds. And why should not crocodiles be acclimatized here in Russia? If the waters of the Neva are too cold for these interesting strangers, there are ponds in our capital, and streams and lakes on the outskirts. Why, for instance, should crocodiles not be bred at Pargolovo or Pavlovsk, or, in Moscow, in the Presnensky Ponds or the Samotyoka

River? Not only could they provide tasty and wholesome fare for our refined gastronomes, they might also serve as a source of entertainment for the ladies who stroll round the ponds, and a lesson in natural history for their children. The crocodile skins could be used to make jewel cases, portmanteaux, cigarette cases and pocketbooks, and many thousands of Russian roubles in the form of those greasy banknotes so beloved of our merchants might find themselves laid by in crocodile skin. We hope to return to this interesting topic many times in the future.'

Although I had been expecting something of the sort, the wild inaccuracy of this news item startled me. Finding no one with whom to share my impressions, I turned to Prokhor Savvich, who sat opposite me, and whom I had observed watching me for a long time. He was holding a copy of *The Shout*, apparently waiting to pass it to me. Silently he took *The Leaflet* from me and handed me *The Shout*, firmly marking with his fingernail the article he wanted me to see. Prokhor Savvich was a very strange individual, a taciturn old bachelor who had not made friends with any of us, hardly spoke to anyone in the office, always had his own opinions about everything, but could not bear to share them with anyone. He lived alone; hardly any of us had ever visited him at home.

Here is the article he pointed out to me in *The Shout*: 'It is universally known that we are a progressive and humane nation, eager to match Europe in this respect. Yet despite all our exertions, and the efforts of this paper, we are still a long way from attaining maturity, as can be seen from a shocking incident that took place in the Arcade yesterday—an event we ourselves had foretold. A foreigner has arrived in our capital, bringing with him a crocodile which he has put on public display in the Arcade. We hastened to welcome this new instance of a salutary enterprise—something sadly lacking in our mighty and richly varied fatherland. But yesterday afternoon at half past four, the foreign proprietor's booth was visited by an individual of extraordinary girth, in an intoxicated state, who paid for his admission and immediately, without the least warning, climbed into the crocodile's jaws. The crocodile was naturally forced to swallow him, if only for self-preservation and to avoid being choked. Tumbling into the crocodile's interior, the unknown individual at once proceeded to fall asleep. Neither the shouts of the animal's foreign owner, nor the screams of his terrified family, nor threats to call the police, made the slightest impression on him. All that could be heard from inside the crocodile was laughter and menaces to hit the crocodile with sticks (*sic*), while the poor mammal, forced to swallow this enormous mass, now shed bitter tears in vain. An uninvited guest is worse than a Tartar, says the proverb; but this insolent visitor refused to leave. We are at a loss to explain such a barbarous incident, which proves immaturity as a nation and besmirches us in the eyes of foreigners. The recklessness of the Russian character has found worthy expression here. What, we ask ourselves, was the uninvited guest seeking? A warm, cosy home? But our capital possesses numerous fine houses containing inexpensive and extremely comfortable apartments, with running water piped from the Neva and gaslit staircases, and frequently with a hall porter provided by the management. We further draw our readers' attention to the barbarous treatment of a domestic animal in this case: the visiting crocodile would naturally find it difficult to digest such a great mass all at once, so here he now lies, swollen to a mountainous size, suffering unbearable agonies as he awaits death. In Europe, cruelty to domestic animals has long been pursued by law. Yet notwithstanding European enlightenment, European pavements and European domestic architecture, we are still a long way from relinquishing our time-honoured prejudices.

'*The houses are new, but the prejudices old . . .*

' . . . and in point of fact not even the houses are new, or at least their staircases are not. This newspaper has repeatedly pointed out that on the Petersburg Side, in the house of the merchant Lukyanov, the steps of the wooden staircase have rotted and split, and have long presented a danger to Afimya Skapidarova, a soldier's wife who is in service with him, and who is obliged to make frequent trips up those stairs carrying water or armfuls of firewood. Our warnings have finally been proved true: yesterday evening, at eight thirty p.m., soldier's wife Afimya Skapidarova fell while carrying a bowl of soup, and broke her leg. We do not know whether Lukyanov is now proposing to repair his staircase; a Russian is often wise after the event, but this Russian's victim has by now no doubt been carried off to hospital. Nor will we tire of repeating that the yard porters who sweep the dirt off the wooden pavements on the Vyborg Side ought not to bespatter the feet of passers-by, but ought to pile the mud in little heaps, as is done in Europe when boots are cleaned. Et cetera, et cetera.'

'What's all this?' I demanded, staring at Prokhor Savvich in some perplexity. 'How can they say such things?'

'What do you mean?'

'Well, I ask you . . . Instead of being sorry for Ivan Matveich, they're being sorry for the crocodile.'

'And why not? They're feeling pity for an animal too, a *mammal*! So how are we worse than Europe, after that? They care a lot about crocodiles there too. He-he-he!'

After which pronouncement, Prokhor Savvich buried himself in his papers and did not say another word.

I put *The Shout* and *The Leaflet* in my pocket, and also gathered up all the back numbers of *The Petersburg News* and *The Shout* that I could find, to entertain Ivan Matveich that evening. And although the evening was still far away, on this occasion I slipped out of the office early, so as to get to the Arcade and have a look, even from a distance, at what was going on there, and to hear different people's remarks and opinions. I foresaw that there would be quite a crush, and for safety's sake I turned up my coat collar to hide my face, for I felt a little bashful. So unused are we to publicity! But I feel I have no right to talk about my own prosaic feelings in the face of such a remarkable and unique event.

THE HEAVENLY CHRISTMAS TREE

I AM A NOVELIST, and I suppose I must have made up this particular story. Why do I say 'I suppose'? I know perfectly well that I made it up; but I keep having the feeling that it really did happen somewhere, sometime, just as I tell it, on Christmas Eve, in a great city, during a terrible frost.

I seem to see a boy in a cellar: he's a very little boy, six years old or even younger. This boy woke up one morning in the cold, damp cellar. He was wearing a little smock and shivering with cold. His breath came out in puffs of white vapour, and as he sat on a trunk in the corner, he was so bored, he started blowing steam out of his mouth and watching it float away. But he was terribly hungry. Several times that morning he had gone over to the bunk where his sick mother lay on a mattress as thin as a pancake, with a bundle under her head for a pillow. How had she ended up there?

She will probably have arrived from some other town with her little boy, and suddenly fallen ill. The landlady of the doss house had been taken off by the police two days before; the other lodgers had wandered out to celebrate the holiday, all but one solitary layabout who had been sprawled there dead drunk for a night and a day, without even having waited for the holiday. In another corner of the room lay an eighty-year-old woman, once a children's nurse but now left to die on her own, moaning and groaning with rheumatism, grousing and grumbling at the little boy, so that he had become too scared to go near her. He had found some water to drink in an outer room, but he couldn't find a crust of bread anywhere. Ten times over he had gone to try to wake his mother. The darkness was getting really frightening. Dusk had fallen long ago, but no one had come to light the lamps. He felt his mother's face and was surprised to find that she didn't move, and had grown as cold as the wall. 'It's really cold here,' he thought, and stood there a while, forgetting that his hand was still resting on the dead woman's shoulder. Then he breathed on his fingers to warm them, and felt around on the bunk for his little cap. Quietly he groped his way out of the cellar. He would have gone earlier, but he was afraid of the big dog at the top of the stairs, which had been howling at the neighbour's door all day. Now the dog had gone, and he could get out into the street.

Lord, what a town! Never in his life had he seen anything like it. Where he's from, the nights are so pitch-black—there's just one lamp for the whole street. The little low houses have their shutters up; after dusk there isn't a soul on the street, people shut themselves away in their houses, and whole packs of dogs come out, hundreds and thousands of them, howling and barking all night. But it used to be so warm there, and he would get food to eat, while here—oh Lord, if only he could eat something! And the rumbling and thumping noises, and so much light, and so many people and horses and carts—and the freezing cold, the freezing cold! Frozen steam billowing up from the hurrying horses, out of their hot, panting mouths; hooves ringing on the cobblestones under the powdery snow, and everyone shoving and jostling, and Lord, he's so hungry, if only he could get just a mouthful of something, and his little fingers are beginning to hurt so. A policeman walked past, looking away so as not to see the boy.

And here was another street—oh, how wide it was! He was sure to be run over here. How they were all shouting, and running and driving along, and how bright it was, so bright! And what's this? Ooh, what a big pane of glass, and behind the glass there's a room, and in the room there's a tree reaching up to the ceiling. It's a fir tree, with so many lights on it, and gold paper, and apples, and there are dolls round it, and little horses, and children running about the room, all neat and tidy, laughing and playing, eating and drinking. Here's a girl who has started dancing with a boy—what a pretty girl she is! And there's music, you can hear it through the glass. The boy stares in wonder, in fact he's laughing, but his very toes are beginning to ache, and his fingers have turned quite red, they won't bend, and they hurt if he moves them.

Suddenly the boy remembers how painful his fingers and toes are; bursting into tears, he runs on. Now he comes to another window and sees another room, and there are trees here too, and tables as well, with pastries, all kinds of pastries—almond ones, red ones, yellow ones, and four rich young ladies sitting there, and whenever anyone comes in, they offer them pastries, and the door keeps opening every minute, lots of fine people are coming in off the street to visit them—the boy crept closer, and all of a sudden he opened the door and went in. Oh, how they all yelled and flapped their hands at him! One of the young ladies hurried over, pressed a kopek into his hand and opened the street door to put him out. How frightened he was! But the coin fell out of his hand and tinkled as it rolled down the steps; his reddened fingers couldn't bend to grasp it.

The boy ran out and hurried off as quickly as he could, with no idea where he was going. Now he feels like bursting into tears again, but he's frightened, and just runs on and on, blowing on his fingers. And he's overcome with misery, suddenly feeling so lonely and scared—but good Lord, what's this now? Here's a crowd of people staring through a window in amazement, and inside there are three dolls, little ones, all dressed up in red and green dresses, and looking just exactly as though they were alive! There's a little old man sitting there playing a big violin, and two other men standing nearby and playing little fiddles, and all nodding their heads in time, and looking at one another, and their lips are moving, they're talking, they're really talking—only you can't hear them through the glass. At first the boy thought they were alive, but then, when he realized they were puppets, he burst out laughing. He'd never seen puppets like that—he didn't even know they existed. And although he felt like crying, those puppets were so, so funny.

Suddenly he felt someone grab hold of him by his smock. A big, bad boy was standing next to him, and without warning he hit him on the head, snatched off his cap, and tripped him up with his foot. The little boy crashed to the ground, and people started shouting. Numb with terror, he jumped up and ran away, and ran and ran. He had no idea where he was going, but found himself running through a gate into someone's yard. He crouched down behind a woodpile. 'They won't find me here; besides, it's dark.'

He sat there, huddled up, breathless with fright, and suddenly, quite suddenly, he felt so happy: his hands and feet stopped hurting, and he felt so warm, as warm as if he was lying on a stove; he gave a shudder: yes, he had almost fallen asleep! How good it would be to sleep here! 'I'll stay sitting here for a bit, and then go back and look at the dolls,' thought the boy, grinning as he remembered them—'just as though they were alive!' And all at once he seemed to hear his mother singing to him. 'Mama, I'm sleeping—oh, how nice it is, sleeping here!'

'Come and see my Christmas tree, little boy,' a quiet voice whispered above him.

At first he thought this was his mama again, but it wasn't her. He couldn't see who had called him, but someone bent over him and hugged him in the dark, and he stretched out his hands, and . . . and all of a sudden—oh, what a bright light! Oh, what a Christmas tree! No, it couldn't be a fir tree—he had never seen such a tree in his life! Where can he be now? Everything is glittering, everything is shining, and there are dolls all around;—but no, they're boys and girls, but so bright and shining, they're circling around him, they're flying in the air, and they're all kissing him, and taking him up and carrying him along with them—and he's flying himself, and now he can see his mama watching him, and laughing with joy at him.

'Mama! Mama! Oh, how nice it is here, Mama!' the boy calls out to her, and kisses the other children again, and he wants to tell them straight away about those dolls in the window. 'Who are you, boys? Who are you, girls?' he asks, laughing with them and loving them.

'This is Christ's Christmas tree,' they tell him. 'Christ always has a Christmas tree on this day, for the little children who haven't got one of their own.' And he discovered that all these boys and girls had been children just like himself, but some of them had frozen to death in the very baskets in which they had been abandoned, on staircases in front of the doors of Petersburg officials; others had been boarded out to Finnish women by the foundlings' hospital, and been suffocated; others had died at their starved mothers' withered breasts during the Samara famine; yet others had choked on the poisonous air in third-class railway carriages; but now they were all here, all of them like angels, all of them in Christ's care, and he himself was one of them, holding out his hands to them and blessing them and their sinful mothers . . . And the mothers of these children were all standing there too, to one side, and weeping; each one knew her little boy or girl, and the children would fly up to them and kiss them, and dry their tears with their little hands, and beg them not to cry, because they were so happy here.

Down below, next morning, the porters found the little body of the boy who had taken refuge behind the woodpile and frozen to death there; and they found his mother too . . . she had died before him. And mother and child found each other again before God in heaven.

But why did I make up this story, so out of place in an ordinary rational diary, and a writer's diary at that? When I had promised to tell stories about real events? But that's just it—I keep imagining that all this could really have happened, I mean what happened in the cellar and behind the woodpile. As for the bit about Christ's Christmas tree—I don't know what to say: could it have happened or not? That's why I'm a novelist—I make up stories.

THE PEASANT MAREY

BUT I THINK all these *professions de foi* are very boring to read; so I am going to tell a certain story, or not even a story, but just a particular distant memory which I'm very keen to recall, for some reason, right here and now, to round off this treatise on the Russian people. I was just nine at the time . . . no, I'd better start with when I was twenty.

It was the second day of Holy Week. The air was warm, the sky was blue, the sun high in the sky, shining warm and bright; but my heart was very heavy. I wandered behind the barrack huts, staring at the palings of the stout prison fence, counting them off—but I didn't even feel like counting them, though I was in the habit of doing that. It was the second day of the prison 'holiday': the convicts were not being taken out to labour; there were crowds of drunk men, and loud abuse and constant quarrels breaking out all over the place. Foul, disgusting songs, gamblers playing cards on the floor by the bunks, and several half-dead convicts, sentenced by their fellows to be beaten up for excessive violence, who were now lying on their bunks covered with sheepskins till they recovered and came round. Already, several times, knives had been drawn. I had found all this, over the first two days of the holiday, so excruciatingly depressing that it made me ill. I had always been revolted by drunken rampages, and more than ever in this place. On these particular days the guards never looked in on the prison at all; there were no searches, no hunts for vodka—they realized that even these outcasts had to be given their heads, just once a year, otherwise things would get even worse. Eventually my heart blazed up in fury. I met M—cki, a Polish political, who gave me a sour look. His eyes flashed, his lips trembled. '*Je hais ces brigands!*' he muttered through gritted teeth as he walked on. I went back to my barrack hut, though only a quarter of an hour before I had rushed out of it like a maniac when six stalwart peasants hurled themselves as one man at Gazin, a drunk Tartar, to shut him up. They set about beating him up, but they were doing it stupidly: their blows could have killed a camel, but they knew that this Hercules would be hard to kill, so they didn't hold back. Now, as I came to my hut, I looked down to the far end and saw Gazin lying on the corner bunk, unconscious and barely showing a sign of life. He had a sheepskin over him, and the men walked round him in silence. They were confident that he would come round by next morning, but even so— you never knew, if the man was unlucky he might die from a beating like that.

I went along to my own bunk, by a window with an iron grille over it, lay down on my back with my hands behind my head, and shut my eyes. I liked lying like that: a sleeping man gets left alone, and meanwhile one can think and dream. But I couldn't dream: my heart was beating uneasily, and M—cki's words were echoing in my ears: *Je hais ces brigands!* But why describe my impressions: even now at night I sometimes dream about those times, and those are my most agonizing dreams of all. Readers may notice that up till now I have scarcely ever spoken of my own prison life in print. Fifteen years ago I wrote *Notes from the House of the Dead* in the voice of an invented character, a criminal who had killed his wife. I might add in passing that since then many people have thought, and still maintain to this day, that I was sentenced to a prison camp for murdering my wife.

Gradually I lapsed into forgetfulness, and my mind strayed off into memories. All through my four years of imprisonment, I would constantly remember my past life, so that it felt as if I had lived through the whole of that life a second time. These memories rose up of their own accord; only rarely would I deliberately call them up. They would start from some minor point, a small detail, sometimes unnoticed, and little by little grow into a whole picture, a powerful and complete impression. I would analyse those impressions, adding new details to what I had lived through long ago, and most importantly, I was constantly correcting the picture—that was my main amusement. On this occasion I suddenly recalled, for some reason, an insignificant moment from my early childhood, when I was just nine: a moment that I might have completely forgotten, but at that time I was particularly fond of those memories of my earliest childhood.

I remembered one August day in the country, a day that was dry and bright but rather cold and windy. Summer was on the way out, and soon we'd have to go back to Moscow for me to spend a boring winter at my French lessons, and I was so sad to leave the country. I walked past the threshing floor, down into a gully, and up to a dense thicket on the far side of it which stretched as far as the woodland. Here I advanced deeper into the bushes; not far off, about thirty paces away, I could hear a solitary peasant ploughing the meadow. I knew that he was moving up a steep hill and the horse was having trouble climbing the slope; every now and then his cries of 'Giddy up!' would float over to me. I know almost all our peasants, but I don't know which of them is ploughing here, nor do I care; I'm deep in my own affairs, for I'm busy too. I'm breaking off a hazel switch to whip the frogs with. Hazel twigs are so pretty, and so flimsy—not like birch twigs at all. I'm interested in bugs and beetles as well, and I collect them: there are some very fine ones, and I also like the nimble little red-and-yellow lizards with their black spots, but I'm afraid of snakes. Though there are far fewer snakes around than lizards. There aren't many mushrooms here; for mushrooms you have to go into the birch wood, and I mean to go there. There was nothing in the world I liked so much as the wood with its mushrooms and wild berries, its insects and birds, hedgehogs and squirrels, and my favourite smell, the damp smell of rotting leaves.

Suddenly the deep silence was broken—I heard, clearly and distinctly, a cry of 'Wolf!' I shrieked, and ran, petrified with terror and yelling at the top of my voice, out onto the meadow and straight up to the peasant ploughing there.

It was our peasant Marey. I don't know if such a name exists, but everyone called him Marey. A stockily built peasant of around fifty, quite tall, with a striking grey streak in his thick dark-brown beard. I knew him, but I had scarcely ever happened to speak to him. He pulled up his horse when he heard my cries, and when I reached him at full tilt, grabbing his plough with one hand and his sleeve with the other, he could see how frightened I was.

'There's a wolf!' I panted at the top of my voice.

Instinctively he raised his head and looked round, almost believing me for a second.

'Where's the wolf?'

'They shouted . . . Someone just shouted "Wolf!"' I stammered.

'Get along, get along, how could there be a wolf? You imagined it! Look around—how could there be a wolf here?' he said quietly and reassuringly. But I was still trembling with fear, and clung even tighter to his smock. I must have been very white too. He looked at me with an anxious smile, evidently fearful and alarmed on my account.

'Dear, dear, what a fright you've had!' he said, shaking his head. 'That'll do, little one! Dear, dear!'

He stretched out his hand and suddenly stroked my cheek.

'There, there, that'll do, Christ be with you, cross yourself now.' But I didn't cross myself. The corners of my mouth were twitching, and I think that must have particularly struck him. He slowly extended one plump earthy finger with a blackened nail, and gently touched my trembling lips.

'Well I never, dearie me,'—and he smiled a slow, almost motherly smile. 'Lord above, look at you, goodness me, dear dear!'

Eventually I realized that there was no wolf, and I had imagined that cry of 'Wolf!' It really had been a very clear and distinct cry, but once or twice in the past I had seemed to hear cries like that (and not only about wolves), and I knew that I had imagined them. (Later on, as I grew older, those hallucinations left me.)

'Well, I'll be off,' I said, with a shy, questioning look at him.

'Very well, then, run along, and I'll watch you from here. I won't let the wolf get you!' he added, still with that motherly smile. 'All right, Christ go with you, off you go'—and he made the sign of the cross over me and himself. I went off, looking back almost every ten steps. As I went, Marey stayed standing there beside his horse, watching me go and giving me a nod every time I looked back. I must confess I was a little embarrassed at having been so frightened, but on I went, still very scared of the wolf, until I reached the first barn halfway up the slope of the hollow. Then all my fear vanished, and suddenly our yard dog Volchok appeared from heaven knows where and rushed up to me. With Volchok by my side I felt perfectly safe, and turned round to Marey for the last time. I couldn't make out his face clearly any more, but I felt that he was still smiling at me with the same gentle look, nodding his head. I waved to him, he waved back and started his little mare.

'Giddy up!' I heard his cry in the distance once more, and the mare tugged at the plough again.

All this came back to me at once, I don't know why; and I recalled it in astonishingly accurate detail. I pulled myself together and sat up on my bunk, and I remember that I found myself still smiling at the memory. I went on remembering it for another minute.

When I got home from Marey that day, I told no one about my 'adventure'. What sort of adventure was it, anyway? And I very soon forgot Marey too. On the few occasions when I met him after that, I never spoke to him—not about the wolf, nor anything else. And yet now, twenty years later in Siberia, I remembered that whole episode so clearly, down to the last detail. So it had taken root in my heart of its own accord, unnoticed and with no help from me; and now it had come back to me when I needed it, and I remembered that poor serf's gentle, motherly smile, and the way he made the sign of the cross, and shook his head: 'Dear, dear, what a fright you've had, little one!' And especially that plump, earthy finger which he softly, timidly and tenderly brought up to touch me on my quivering lips. Of course, anyone would have cheered up the child, but here, in this solitary encounter, something quite different seemed to have happened. Even if I had been his own son, he couldn't have looked at me with eyes that shone with greater love. What forced him to do that? He was our property, our own peasant and serf, and I was his little master. No one would ever know how gentle he had been to me, nor reward him for it. Could he have just been so fond of very little children? Some are. We were on our own when we met in that empty meadow, and only God on high, perhaps, could look down and see what deep, humane, enlightened feeling, what delicate, almost feminine tenderness could fill the heart of a coarse, brutally uncouth Russian serf, with no expectations nor any inkling of his coming freedom. Tell me—was this not what Konstantin Aksakov had in mind when he wrote about the high degree of culture in our common people?

And now, climbing down from my bunk and looking round me, I remember I suddenly felt that I could see these unhappy wretches with new eyes. In that moment, by some miracle, all the hatred and fury was lifted from my heart. I walked on, looking closely at the faces that I met. This shaven-headed, disgraced, tipsy peasant, with a convict's brand on his face, with his hoarse voice bellowing a drunken song—he could be that very same Marey; I couldn't look into his heart. That evening I met M——cki again. Poor man! He couldn't have any memories of peasants like Marey, nor any view of these people, beyond *Je hais ces brig-ands!* No, those Polish prisoners had more to bear than I did.